HERO AMICUS CURIAE

More books by Suzan Harden

(Each series is in suggested reading order)

Bloodlines

Blood Magick
Zombie Love
Zombie Confidential
Zombie Wedding
Amish, Vamps & Thieves
Blood Sacrifice
Love, War & a Bulldog
Zombie Goddess
Ravaged
Sacrificed
Reality Bites
Ghouls in the Grocery Store
Resurrected
Bloodlines Shorts Anthology
Bloodline: The First Boxed Set

Seasons of Magick

Spring
Summer
Autumn
Winter
The Seasons of Magick Anthology

Justice

Sword and Sorceress 28 ("Justice")
Sword and Sorceress 30 ("Diplomacy in the Dark")
Justice: The Beginning
A Question of Balance
A Modicum of Truth
A Matter of Death
A Touch of Mother
A Twist of Love
A Virtue of Child
A Hand of Father
A Measure of Knowledge

The Justice Thalia Stories
Snowfall
Murder Most Fowl
The Sweetest Poison

888-555-HERO
Hero De Facto
Hero Ad Hoc
Hero De Novo
A Very Hero Christmas
Hero De Jure
Hero In Camera
Hero Amicus Curiae
A Very Hero Wedding
Hero Ad Litem

Solar Systems Services, Inc.
Alone is Not Lonely

Millersburg Magick Mysteries
Spells and Sleuths
Fae and Felonies
Magick and Murder

Soccer Moms of the Apocalypse
Pestilence in Pumpkin Spice (Coming Soon)
Famine In French Vanilla
War in White Chocolate
Death in Double Mocha

Miscellaneous
Sword and Sorceress 31 ("Pig-Headed")
Sword and Sorceress 32 ("Unexpected")
Practical Witches
Revenge Served Hot
The Yule Switch

For updates, news, and giveaways, join Suzan's mailing list or visit her website at www.suzanharden.com. You can also check her out on Twitter or Facebook.

For Stella and Emma,
two of the most awesome Brits I know

HERO AMICUS CURIAE (888-555-HERO #7)
Copyright 2021 by Suzan Harden
All rights reserved
ISBN: 978-1-938745-93-5

Published by Angry Sheep Publishing
Findlay, Ohio

Interior Design by JW Manus
Cover Design by For the Muse Designs

HERO AMICUS CURIAE

888-555-HERO #7

SUZAN HARDEN

CHAPTER 1

Susan Kennedy slammed down her phone receiver and roared, "Harri!" Fury ignited every cell in her body, a fury not even the sweet floral scent of the chamomile tea on her desk could soothe. She shoved back her chair, stomped across her office floor, and grabbed the papers she had printed off during her phone call from the multipurpose machine. For once, she was glad she'd accepted the partnership at Winters and Franklin. She didn't care about her name on the letterhead. It was more satisfying to have someone to share the rage with. She yanked open her office door to find the law firm's intern Steve Connors reaching for the knob.

"You okay?"

"No! I'm pissed!"

He stepped back, not out of fear. The kid was a super after all, and smart enough to go to law school instead of joining the underwear crowd as the firm's senior partner put it. Susan charged down the short hallway to the reception area with Steve following. "Harri!"

Harri's office door was wide open, and their legal assistant Patty Ames wasn't sitting at the reception desk. Instead, their IT guru Arthur Drallhickey perched on the chair with wide eyes and the receiver at his ear. "She's in a meeting at the moment," he said to whoever was on the other end of the line while he pointed towards the breakroom.

Harriet "Harri" Winters stepped out into the reception area from the breakroom with a steaming mug at the same moment Aisha Franklin poked her head around the edge of her own office door.

"What the hell is going on out here?" Harri said.

"One moment, please." Arthur jabbed a button on the phone console. "Would you mind taking this to another room? There's a client on the phone, and she can hear everything you say."

Susan blew out a deep breath. "Sorry, Arthur."

Harri inclined her head toward Aisha's office.

Susan trooped into the room after her. The anger burned itself out with Arthur's reminder of propriety. It was bad when a former supervillain showed the most decorum out of everyone in the building.

Once Steve closed the door behind him, Harri slurped her coffee before she said, "Start from the beginning."

"I just got off the phone with Mother Defiant." Susan crossed her arms to keep from shaking thanks to the adrenaline rush draining away. "She was served this morning. Right in the middle of her stopping Professor Geode from stealing the new meteorite at the Museum of Natural History."

"Well, that's either the bravest or the dumbest process server in history," Harri muttered.

"Who sued her and why?" Aisha asked.

Susan eyed her. "Our former employer."

Harri choked on her coffee. Brown cinnamon-scented liquid

sprayed everywhere. Between one blink and the next, the shades in Aisha's office closed, and Steve held a wad of paper towels full of coffee splatters. And probably spit. Susan didn't want to think too much about the second.

She grabbed Aisha's waste can and held it out for Steve. He dropped the nasty towels into the receptacle. She eyed the kid. "It's a good thing you're not a germophobe."

He grinned. "You learn to ignore certain things when you see the world differently."

Aisha dropped into her office chair. "I've been waiting for them to try something since I quit. I'm just surprised it took them over a year."

"They stole Mother Defiant from me last summer to begin with." Susan unfolded her arms and held out the sheaf to Aisha. "Why are they pulling this crap now?"

Harri was too busy trying to clear coffee droplets from her trachea with some extreme coughing to comment. Steve dashed out of the office and returned with a bottle of water from the break room. He traded her cup for his bottle.

Aisha flipped through the copy of the lawsuit and frowned. "We aren't named as defendants. I thought for sure they'd go for a tortious interference in a contract complaint against the firm."

"I made sure Mother Defiant crossed her 't's and dotted her 'i's before we signed her," Harri croaked. "Besides, they can always amend the complaint."

"Well, they can't touch Winters and Franklin without us filing a cross-complaint over how they used Mother Defiant to plant that virus on my phone and thereby infecting your computers," Susan said.

"Assuming we can prove it," Harri said. "We still don't know for sure if Dewey and Cheatham were behind it, or if Corvus used them, too."

"Come on." Susan gestured sharply. "You said yourself Howard Dewey did everything but admit he was in bed with Corvus."

"You know there's a huge difference between knowing something and proving it to a judge or jury's satisfaction," Harri growled.

"The alternative for Howard appears to be going after our clients instead." Aisha grimaced before she looked at Susan again. "Let me guess. Mother Deception wants you to handle this personally." She handed the complaint and initial discovery request to Harri who scanned them.

"Yeah." Susan grinned. "I think Harri scares her even more than you do."

"I scare her?" Aisha's right eyebrow rose.

"Now that she knows your alter ego." Susan shrugged. Aisha being a superhero herself meant the firm had to acknowledge her secret identity to their clients so there wasn't a question of conflict of interest.

Which was part of the reason any client went through an extremely thorough vetting process prior to being accepted by the firm.

Harri looked up from the copies of the complaint. "Go to Hermanville, talk Mother Defiant down, and file the answer. This is a nuisance suit."

"That's exactly the point." Susan gestured in the direction of the federal courthouse here in Canyon Pointe. "Carol Inunza's arraignment is tomorrow. You really think they're not going to use that against us? Divide and conquer."

"Look, we already know we can't handle her defense—"

"And we can't find any of our friends crazy enough to take her on as a client either," Aisha muttered as she glared at Harri.

"No." Susan slashed her hand. "We are not rehashing whether or not Harri should have pressed charges against Carol."

Aisha jabbed a finger in Harri's direction. "Don't tell me you actually agree with her—"

"Stop," Harri growled. "Just stop. Susan needs to sooth Mother Defiant's feathers, which means one of us needs to deal with Carol in the morning. Have you ever handled an arraignment before?"

"Not since Captain Mojave's DUI when I first joined Dewey and Cheatham." Aisha sighed. "That was only because Howard Dewey was in the U.S. Virgin Islands with his then-current girlfriend, and I got thrown in the deep end to see if I could swim."

"You're nominated to replace Susan," Harri said. "Because I've never done one, and Carol needs competent representation."

"You're the one who thinks Carol didn't kidnap her, Little Miss Stockholm Syndrome," Aisha snapped.

"Which is exactly why you need to do it," Harri said.

Something smelled a little fishy. Susan frowned. "What's the real reason you don't want to handle the arraignment?"

Harri's cheeks flushed. "It's got nothing to do with Carol."

"Or maybe it has something to do with the prosecutor." Aisha leaned her elbows on her desktop. "Please don't tell me you and Jim Duncan hooked up—"

"Excuse me?" Harri grimaced. "That was Jeremy."

"You and Judge Castillo?" Steve blurted.

Harri's blush went from pink to red. "It was one date," she muttered. "It didn't end well, so you need to handle the arraignment, Aisha. My past is not going to help Carol, and I can't get Castillo to recuse himself over a sucky date."

"Unless you want to go to Hermanville in my place?" Susan raised both hands in a balancing gesture. "But I can guarantee Mother Defiant will throw a fit."

"I thought she was scared of me," Aisha said sourly

"Doesn't mean she won't bitch." Susan shrugged.

Aisha sighed again. "Fine. Can you run through the points of Carol's arraignment with me before you take off?"

"Of course."

"Good." Harri nodded sharply. "That's taken care of." She strode out of the office.

Steve shook his head before he turned back to the other two women. "Harri never struck me as the one-night stand type."

"I wouldn't say anything about it outside of this office." Susan smirked. "She'd make Arthur design a weapon that could take you out."

CHAPTER 2

The next morning, Aisha Franklin sat beside Carol Inunza at the defendant's table in one of Canyon Pointe's federal district criminal courtrooms, wondering how the hell she let her law partners talk her into temporarily representing Carol. Even though Harri had refused to press charges against Carol for kidnapping her, their fellow attorney couldn't escape the charges for aiding and abetting the prison break of four inmates from Mauvaises, the federal maximum security prison specifically for those convicts classified as supervillains.

Part of the problem of finding a criminal defense attorney willing to represent Carol was having a member of the bar become a minion. The other part was Carol's husband Pablo was one of the top criminal judges in the state. No one wanted to be in front of him if they lost his wife's case.

"I still don't understand why you're doing this," Carol murmured. She wore an orange two-piece outfit and had what Harri referred to as "jail stink". Aisha had never noticed the odor before she had superpowers. Harri claimed Aisha's smoking back then had deadened her nose to the funk. But with the super senses her mother-in-law gifted her, the scent was a million times worse than a skunk.

"Because your husband did me a solid when Mike Michaels had Harri arrested on trumped up charges," Aisha said. The former Canyon Pointe D.A. was now doing his own residency in the state pen for corruption and fraud.

"Pablo wouldn't do a 'favor' for anyone with a case in his court," Carol whispered. "He follows the law. Always." And she was right. Pablo Inunza had a perfect reputation as a criminal court judge.

Until his wife was arrested. Now Aisha's ex-husband Calvin Johnson, one of the few assistant D.A.s to survive the Michaels purge, headed the city's district attorneys office. Cal didn't have a choice but to investigate Judge Inunza because the jurist had made a lot of enemies, and the mayor and city council were embarrassed as hell after their pledge to clean up Canyon Pointe with what their predecessors had done.

"Right now, I'm thinking you should have followed in his footsteps," Aisha hissed back.

She looked over her shoulder at the people in the gallery. Other attorneys, family members, and prisoners waited their turn with the judge. But there was also plenty of news people in attendance as well. Carol, an esteemed attorney in her own right, and her involvement with the prison break had stirred up a hornet's nest of attention.

She turned back to Carol. "Where are your husband and son?"

"I asked them not to come." Carol stared at the cuffs on her wrists.

"That's not helping your case." Aisha forced her fingers to relax. She didn't need to crush another pen and ruin another suit. "Even I know family support can make a difference in a defendant's case."

"I've caused them both enough trouble." Carol looked up. Unshed tears shimmered in her cinnamon brown eyes. "Or are you going to BS me and say Pablo's not under investigation because of what I did?"

"I wouldn't lie to you about something like that," Aisha murmured. "However, we need to focus on you at the moment."

Carol shook her head sadly. "I'm just glad Paul is out of high school. Can you imagine what hateful things the other kids would say to him?"

Aisha could imagine very well what would happen. She, Harri, and Jeremy had gotten enough crap for far less when they were children.

"Hi, Aisha!"

Distracted from her maudlin thoughts, she looked up at Jim Duncan's cheery greeting. The federal prosecutor was still as good-looking as he had been in law school. He was a sweetheart in life, but in the courtroom, he was a freaking bull shark. She was kind of glad she was only handling the arraignment.

"Hey, Jim."

"Can we talk for a moment?" He inclined his head toward the empty jury box.

"Of course." She turned to Carol. "I'll be right back." She stood and strode over to Jim.

He lowered his voice. "My boss is refusing to offer a plea deal."

"My client cooperated and spilled everything she knows about Miss Purrception and Trubble," Aisha whispered back.

"She's also a member of the bar in a city that had a huge scandal in the D.A. and mayor's offices last year." Jim crossed his arms.

"These are federal charges," Aisha protested.

"I'm aware of who I work for," he said dryly. "If it helps, I believe Carol thought she was protecting her husband and son. But let's face it, she kidnapped Harri and planned to murder Trubble. I can't get a plea deal to fly. Not right now."

"Did you argue the money coming out of the taxpayers' pockets by taking this to trial? Not to mention burying an upstanding judge as collateral damage?"

"Girlfriend, give me a little credit." Jim made a "give me a break" face at her.

"What about bail?"

He shook his head.

Aisha nodded. "Okay. Thanks for trying." She returned to her seat.

"What did he say?" Carol whispered.

"No leeway," Aisha murmured. "His boss thinks your case is a slam dunk as well as you being a flight risk."

"Damn." Carol stared at her shackled wrists. "I'm so screwed if I go to prison."

"Don't give up just yet," Aisha said. "Let's give the judge a chance." Carol was totally right though, but Aisha couldn't give in to despair. She hadn't lied about Carol's chances, but neither could she look at the glass as half-full like Harri did.

However, part of her wished Susan was handling the arraignment. The newest partner had a lot more trial experience. But they needed to look out for Mother Defiant's interests, and the superhero preferred Susan. Harri was right about it being a nuisance suit from Dewey and Cheatham, but maybe they should have sent one of their super clients with Susan to watch her back. Dewey and Cheatham were in bed with the dismantled black ops group Corvus somehow, which made them doubly dangerous.

Carol snorted softly. "I've been in front of Judge Castillo before as an attorney. He likes throwing books at people. Especially attorneys who do dumb shit."

Aisha kept her mouth shut. Insulting her client wasn't going to help the situation. She also didn't want to give Carol false hope, but maybe, just maybe, she could get the judge to recuse himself.

"All rise," the U.S. marshal acting as bailiff called out. "The United States District Court, District of Southern Mojave, is now in session. The Honorable Judge Francis Castillo presiding."

The judge strode into the courtroom, and Aisha took a good look at him. He was medium height with salt and pepper hair and beard. Definitely not Harri's usual type. But if their date was that bad, why didn't Harri come over to Aisha's condo or call her for a post-mortem gripe session?

Castillo's black robes rustled when he dropped heavily into his chair. "Be seated."

For once, Aisha didn't have to nudge her client to stand or sit in court. She wasn't sure if that was a good thing or not.

While everyone resumed their seats, his clerk handed him the first case file, and he flipped it open as he put on his black plastic reading glasses. "The United States versus Inunza."

Aisha, Carol, and Jim stood.

Judge Castillo looked up from the paperwork. He ignored Aisha and Jim, and his attention focused solely on Carol. His expression was a cross between anger and a disappointed dad. Aisha crossed her fingers, praying he would say something, anything, truly stupid, in order for her to move for him to recuse himself from Carol's case.

Alarmed murmurs and the slaps and clicks of soles and heels on the tile came from the hallway. Something was going on outside the courtroom. Aisha turned to look behind her. Instinct said trouble was coming.

"Am I boring you, Counselor?" the judge snapped.

"Sir, I think we need to evacuate the court—" Aisha started.

The bang of the public doors of the courtroom crashing open made everyone look toward the back. A security guard panted. "Judge, we need to clear everyone through your—"

A shot rang out, and the guard collapsed, blood drenching the front of his uniform. Shrieks and shouts from the other attorneys, accused, and spectators filled the air.

Masked people in black rushed inside, armed to the teeth. The lead invader aimed and fired. The bailiff didn't even have a chance to draw his weapon before he went down in a spray of red.

Instinct kicked in. Aisha pulled Carol off her chair and down to the carpet before she covered her client's body with her own.

"Get on the floor!" one of the assailants yelled. Everybody who hadn't done so already, including Judge Castillo, hit the carpet.

Someone poked something metal in Aisha's back. She tensed, waiting for the bullet that would tell the whole world she was a super.

"Are you Aisha Franklin?" a gruff masculine voice said.

She gritted her teeth and raised her hands. Something in her gut said he already knew who she was. "Yes. I'll cooperate. Please don't hurt anyone else."

"Get up," he ordered.

She slowly and carefully got to her feet. The leader was around six feet tall. From the snug and proper way his tactical gear fit, not only did he know exactly what he was doing, there wasn't an ounce of fat under his clothing.

He slammed an item on the defendant's table. "Call the Ghost Owl. We want him in return for the hostages."

Aisha stared at the cheap burner cell phone.

Well, crap. Maybe hiding her superhero identity's gender wasn't such a smart move after all.

CHAPTER 3

Harri Winters resisted the urge to curse and slam down her phone receiver. Instead, she gently set it in its cradle and beat her head against the wood of her secondhand desk a couple of times. The slight pain didn't change a damn thing. None of the criminal defense attorneys she personally knew would touch Carol's case.

At the knock on her office door, she raise her head. Steve poked his head around the edge and frowned.

"Another one said no?"

"How'd you guess?"

A wry smile crossed Steve's face as he entered with two cups of coffee. "The stink of despair and anger, but mainly, the red spot on your forehead." He clicked his tongue. "You've really gotta stop beating your head on the desk, Harri. It's a good way to give yourself a concussion."

"Maybe if I injure myself, someone specializing in criminal defense will take pity and realize I tortured Carol." She gratefully accepted the huge mug with "Lawyers do it with appeal" stenciled on the side. It had been a graduation present from Jeremy, her foster brother and one of her closest friends. She sipped the black coffee and leaned back in her chair.

"I don't suppose you know anyone back home in Seattle who might be interested in making their name, do you?" She tried giving Steve puppy dog eyes. The same expression his twin brother often used on her. Unlike Rey, Steve had an edge to his personality. It would serve him well as an attorney.

"Mom and Dad are heavily in the tech field." He shrugged. "Any attorneys they know are corporate or IP lawyers. Anyone I know is in the same position I am—a first-year student."

Steve took a sip of his own coffee. Plain black java. None of the pixy barf crap Aisha and Patty drank, the fairy pee Susan preferred, or even the cinnamon flavoring Harri herself had become addicted to. The no frills attitude was one of the reasons Harri liked the kid.

Her intercom buzzed, and she tapped the appropriate button. "What's up, Patty?"

"Before you start screaming dirty words in front of the intern, this is a professional call." Their assistant sucked in a deep breath before she added, "Eddie is on line 1."

Harri groaned, but Patty was right. Eddie wouldn't be calling her unless he had to. They'd made their peace since the divorce, but Eddie's new wife Sarah was absolutely convinced Harri was trying to get him back. Besides, why would she want her ex back when she had her own superhero sleeping in her bed?

The button for line 1 started blinking. She took a fortifying drink of her java before she lifted the receiver and jabbed the button. "*Que pasa*, Eddie?"

"This hasn't been released to the press yet, so I need you to keep this between us," he rumbled, but there was an edge to his voice. Whatever he was about to say was personal.

She glanced at Steve before she answered, "You know who lives in our building. There's no such thing as a secret."

"That's why I'm begging you and your crew not to do anything stupid," Eddie snapped.

"When have we—"

"There was the time you nearly drowned in Lake Del Oro," her ex drawled.

Steve winced and Harri wanted to kick Eddie in the samosas. It wasn't the kid's fault Professor Paranoia had taken control of Steve's mind and was using him to trash Rey's reputation as Captain Justice. She had gone after Steve wearing her current boyfriend's superhero togs. After fishing her out of the lake, Aisha threatened to break up the law partnership over Harri's stunt.

And after the near-death experience, even she had to admit it was a stupid move on her part.

Harri cleared her throat. "Do you need one of our clients to suit up?"

"No!" Eddie lowered his voice. "I need you to keep everyone in check. We've got a hostage situation in the federal courthouse with shots fired."

A chill ran through Harri before he finished speaking. Aisha was downtown at that courthouse for Carol's arraignment.

"It's Judge Castillo's courtroom."

Harri's cinnamon coffee threatened to make a reappearance. Aisha would probably survive a point-blank gunshot, but no one else in the courtroom would. Harri didn't know what would be worse, Aisha's guilt over not saving all the hostages or her secret identity being exposed.

CHAPTER 4

Susan guided her rental car into a chain café's drive-thru to pick up bagels, cream cheese, and caffeine on her way to Mother Defiant's apartment. The personal residence seemed the best way to meet with Eugenia without her traipsing around in her superhero togs.

Susan tapped her fingers on the steering wheel in time to the pop song on the radio. Maybe she should broach the subject of opening a satellite office here in the state capital. After they hired a couple of associates, of course.

She rolled up to the speaker and gave her order. She smiled to herself as the girl manning the drive-thru chirped the total. The morning perkiness of the barista would have driven Harri crazier than usual. Susan guided her vehicle around the corner of the building.

A huge black SUV pulled in behind her rental. All she could see in the rearview mirror was the blinding chrome grill.

For an instant, worry ran through her. The sheriff in Bluffton still hadn't discovered who had hired the guys who trashed Mom and Dad's vacation cabin at Christmas. Thankfully, insurance covered most of the damage, and with Mom's advancing dementia, her parents decided to put the cabin on the market. But part of her wondered if the vandalism wasn't retaliation for her joining Winters and Franklin. Harri and Aisha had made some powerful enemies out of not just Corvus, but the shadowy clients who hired them to perform their dirty work.

Which included hers and Aisha's former employers.

Susan never understood why Aisha stayed at Dewey and Cheatham as long as she had. Her new partner was a smart cookie. But then, Aisha probably wasn't pimped out to Captain Mojave like Stuart Cheatham tried to do with Susan.

Joining Winters and Franklin gave her an opportunity to put down some roots. Aisha's husband Rey had some great ideas for revitalizing the Canyon Block that didn't involve gentrification. A little shop to sell her handmade jewelry sounded like a wonderful way to spend her retirement.

The sedan in front of her rental pulled away, and Susan tapped the gas to pull forward to the window. A jolt to her rental was followed by a horrendous *crunch*. The idiot in the SUV had hit her.

"You okay, ma'am?" the young woman at the window asked.

Before Susan could answer, the SUV rammed her rental car again and continued pushing the smaller sedan through the drive-thru and toward the street.

Right into the path of an oncoming semi-truck.

CHAPTER 5

Aisha looked at the burner phone and back at the gunman. If she dialed the Ghost Owl's number, her phone would ring. How could she spin this in a way that wouldn't get everyone in the courtroom dead and her secret identity exposed?

He shifted and pointed the muzzle of his gun at Carol's unprotected back though his gaze remained locked on Aisha. "You've got three seconds, or I start shooting hostages. Three—"

"I'm doing it," she said in the same low, soothing tone she reserved for when Mitch was fussy.

"Two—"

An idea sparked in her brain. She dialed the Ghost Owl's official number. As she expected, a popular hip-hop song came from her purse. The gunman reached in and pulled out her smart phone. He swung the muzzle to point at her chest.

"What kind of game are you playing, bitch?"

"I'm not playing a game."

Harsh laughter erupted from the gunman. "You expect me to believe you're the Ghost Owl?"

She lifted her chin. "He must have forwarded his phone to mine, which means he knows you're here."

"We cut off the cameras to the building," the gunman stated. Aisha could feel his eyes boring into her. "I said no games." He pivoted, aimed at Jim, and pulled the trigger.

She shoved the gunman's arm, and the shot missed, but it ricocheted off a building support pillar and tore through the State of Mojave flag on the right side of the judge's bench before burrowing into the wood above Judge Castillo's vacated chair. The gunman whirled and backhanded Aisha across her face. She moved with the blow and let herself fall backward into her chair so he didn't break his hand.

"Stupid bitch," he muttered and aimed the weapon at her head.

"Stop it!" Carol inserted herself between the gun and Aisha. "You kill her, and I guarantee her clients will rip this building apart to get to you."

"I just want one client in particular," he growled. But Carol's words must have had some effect. He didn't pull the trigger.

"Let me call my partner." Aisha nudged Carol back and carefully stood to look like she was in pain. "She can get him to cooperate. I just handle his merchandising deals."

He waved his gun at Carol. "Sit on the floor." He stepped back and thumbed Aisha's phone. From the ringing, he had hit the speaker function.

On the third ring, Patty chirped, "Law Offices of Winters and Franklin. How may I help you?"

The gunman gestured at Aisha with her phone.

"Hey, Patty. I need to talk to Harri." Aisha glanced at the gunman. "It's really important."

There was a slight gasp from the receiver before Patty answered.

"She's on another call. Give me a second. Also, Eddie wants to know if you'd like to get the babies together for a playdate."

Aisha wanted to sigh in relief, but she didn't dare. After all the crap that had happened over the last year and a half, the firm's personnel had put together a series of codes. Patty had confirmed the FBI knew what was happening at the federal courthouse. Babies referred to calling in any of their superhero clients.

"Do me a favor and tell Eddie we'll make a date for some other time, okay?" Aisha murmured.

"All right, she's off the other call," Patty said. "Putting you through."

The line clicked, and Harri's voice filtered through the speaker. "Hey, girl. Can't handle a little arraignment?"

It was the same fake pleasantry Harri used when she was truly scared. Only someone who knew her would hear the slight tremor in her voice.

"There's some folks—" When the gunman brought his weapon to bear on her again, Aisha swallowed hard. "—here who want to talk to the Ghost Owl. I tried to call him, but he's got his phone forwarded to mine."

"That's weird." Someone whispered in the background before Harri continued, "Let me try one of the alternate contact numbers. Can I call you back in a few minutes?"

Aisha eyed the gunman. He nodded once.

"Yeah, thanks, I appreciate it."

"How did the arraignment go?" Harri asked.

"The judge wants us to work out a plea deal. I'm waiting for an answer from Jim Duncan."

"What are the odds?"

"I'd say forty-seven percent at the moment." Aisha waited for the gunman and his crew to catch what she was really saying, but they didn't seem to think anything unusual was going on.

"Ouch. By the way, Susan wants to move brunch to ten on Saturday. Is that okay with you?"

"Let's just make it noon," Aisha said. "We all know how much you like to sleep in." The gunman motioned for her to end the call. Luckily, she'd already delivered the information law enforcement and the local superheroes would need.

"Okay, let me track down the Ghost Owl, and I'll call you back." Harri hung up.

The gunman slipped her phone into his pocket. "Keep cooperating, Ms. Franklin. You might live to go home."

"And if the Ghost Owl doesn't come?" she asked.

"He's a superhero," the gunman said confidently. "He'll come. They all do."

Aisha hugged herself. At least, Eddie and the FBI knew what they were up against. She just prayed the bad guys wouldn't start shooting the hostages if another superhero showed.

Or Black Falcon wouldn't tear the bad guys limb from limb because they were stupid enough to take his wife prisoner.

CHAPTER 6

Harri replace the receiver of her phone set into its cradle and looked at the three men gathered in her office. "Did you get all of that, Eddie?"

Steve held up his smart phone so her ex-husband could hear her conversation with Aisha. Tim and Arthur stood behind their intern, wearing matching frowns.

"Did I get that right? Forty-seven hostages and a dozen bad guys?" Eddie said.

"That's what my partner said."

There was some FBI discussion at the other end of the line, then a woman spoke. "Ms. Winters, this is Sylvia Consuelo. I'm the new special agent in charge of the Canyon Pointe FBI office. Would the Ghost Owl be willing to work with us to resolve the hostage crisis?"

"The Ghost Owl would be willing to, Special Agent in Charge Consuelo." Harri looked up at Tim who stood behind Steve's chair.

Tim Canyon's family had been one of the founders of Canyon Pointe, just like hers had. But unlike her, Tim lost everything when the so-called superhero Seismic Shift murdered his wife and son and framed him for the crimes. Out of grief, he'd become the vigilante known as the Ghost Owl.

Except he'd retired after Steve nearly killed him when the kid's mind was being controlled by the supervillain Professor Paranoia.

Around the same time, Aisha's mother-in-law made her hormone-related super powers permanent. So Aisha asked Tim if she could use his old moniker. She paid him a licensing fee for the use, so in theory, it was a win-win for everyone.

"Consuelo, can I talk privately with you and Special Agent Lewis?" Harri said. "This edges into attorney-client confidentiality."

"One moment," the head of the local FBI office murmured. There was some shuffling, some rather loud protests, and then the sound of a door closing. "All right, Winters. It's just me and Lewis. I'm assuming from the guilty look on his face the Ghost Owl is one of the hostages."

Damn, Consuelo was quick. Harri glanced at Tim. He nodded. "Yes."

"And the reason he hasn't turned himself over to the intruders?" Consuelo asked.

"The Ghost Owl and Ms. Franklin have reason to believe if he does so, those intruders will kill the hostages," Tim answered.

"To whom am I speaking?" Consuelo asked.

"Our head of security Tim Canyon," Harri said. "He's trained most of our clients in self-defense and criminal detection techniques." She left out the part where Eddie helped with the training. God only knew how much of a hardass Consuelo was.

"You have an acquitted murderer working for you?"

Okay, maybe she was a little bit of a hardass. Tim's ears flared a brilliant red.

"Mr. Canyon was absolved of the accusations last year, Special Agent," Harri said as evenly as she could manage.

There was some whispering at the other end of the line before Consuelo grunted. "Can you get a message to the Ghost Owl?" the special agent in charge asked.

"I doubt it," Harri answered. "We'll give him away if we try, assuming the bad guys haven't confiscated everyone's phones in the courtroom. He probably had just enough time to forward his calls to Aisha's phone."

"So you're stalling?" There was a hint of disbelief in Consuelo's tone.

"Your hostage negotiator has a better chance of convincing them to surrender," Tim said. "With that many hostages and armed intruders, the odds are someone's going to get hurt or killed if you send in supers."

"The intruders have already sealed off the elevators and stairwells for the floor," Eddie volunteered.

"You are not authorized to share that information, Mr. Lewis," Consuelo barked.

Well, that definitely answered the question of whether she was a hardass.

Harri cleared her throat. "Special Agent Consuelo, while I agree with my head of security about giving the FBI negotiators a chance to resolve things, I will need to let my clients know what's going on if the FBI needs assistance."

"I've heard you have a habit of getting in the middle of your clients' lives," Consuelo said.

"Only when I have to, Special Agent," Harri murmured.

"All right, Agent Lewis will fill you in."

Harri resisted the urge to complain about the agent in charge wasting everyone's time. Maybe Consuelo realized Harri wasn't trying to usurp her authority. Or more likely, Consuelo realized she needed patsies if things go south during the hostage negotiations.

"A group of armed assailants entered the Ruth Bader Ginsburg Federal Courthouse at eight-fifty-two this morning," Eddie recited. "They shot three of the security guards and two U.S. marshals. Witnesses gave the number of assailants between six and twenty."

"Aisha can only confirm how many were in the courtroom itself," Harri said. "If it were me, I'd want extra people for lookouts."

"Plus one person to kill the elevators and two more for each of the stairwells," Eddie added.

"Do you know if there were members of this group on the inside?" Tim asked.

"Not yet." Consuelo's voice was crisp. "You wouldn't happen to have a client with x-ray vision, would you?"

"No, but—"

Arthur motioned for Harri to put the call on mute.

"Special Agent, give us a moment." She nodded to Steve.

He thumbed an icon. "Clear."

Arthur turned to Tim. "What if we use the scanner prototype we're working on?"

"What scanner?" Harri frowned at the men.

"An idea Arthur came up with after the incident with Seismic Shift last year. Just in case you got yourself blown up in a building again." Tim scowled at their IT manager. "If we show it to the Feebs, other agencies are going to want a piece."

Arthur shrugged. "Getting the patent for it will be delayed if we don't save our IP attorney." He glanced nervously at Harri. "N-not that you can't handle the patent registration, H-Harri."

After nearly a year and a half since the attack on City Hall, despite the fact that they worked together and lived in the same building, even though she was the godmother to the little girl he raised with his girlfriend, Arthur Drallhickey was still scared of her.

"It's not my invention that may get seized by Uncle Sam." Harri gestured at Arthur and Tim. "Do you think the prototype will tell the FBI the whereabouts of these terrorists?"

Both men nodded.

Harri scrubbed her hands down her face. "I really wish Blue Racer still lived in Canyon Pointe. He and Cobblestone would be the best supers to handle these jerks."

"Not to mention, you still need someone to go in as the Ghost Owl," Tim said.

She held up an index finger. "Don't even think about it."

"I didn't mean me," he growled. "And you're not going either."

She opened her mouth for a retort when Arthur said, "We can argue about this later. The FBI is waiting on us."

Harri motioned for Steve to take his smart phone off mute.

"Special Agent, my tech geniuses have a scanner that may be able to locate the bad guys and the hostages, but I still think you should bring some super help," Harri said.

"My people can handle this without civilians getting involved," Consuelo sneered. "I don't need them destroying a federal building."

"Last year, I would have agreed with you, Special Agent," Harri said. "But my worldview has changed." She smiled at the three men on the other side of her desk. "It's amazing how much being rescued from a deadly three-story fall will do when someone's literally trying to fry you."

In the background, Eddie rumbled something quietly to his boss.

Consuelo exhaled loudly and said, "It depends on who you have in mind, Winters."

"Sourpuss and Nix," Harri said. "Worst case scenario you might have a few broken windows. And we will get someone to go in as the Ghost Owl outfit because that's who the bad guys are expecting."

"Who?" Consuelo demanded.

"Special Agent, would you please give me a chance to make some phone calls before you totally slam my idea?"

"All right," Consuelo drawled. "We'll try it your way. The supers and your people have fifteen minutes to get here." The line clicked and went silent.

Steve thumbed the controls before he slid his phone into the front pocket of his chinos. "When Rey finds out about this—"

Harri's office door slammed open, showing a furious Rey Garcia, still wearing his apron from Marta's. "Rey already knows."

CHAPTER 7

Susan threw the gear into park, stomped on the brake pedal and yanked the emergency brake for all it was worth. Her efforts only slowed the rental sedan's steady movement into oncoming vehicles. The semi driver blew his horn, but there was nowhere for him to go in the heavy morning traffic without making things worse.

The semi clipped the front corner of the rental with a nasty *CRUNCH*. Her vehicle spun around giving her a good view of the SUV and its driver. He wore a knit cap despite the summer heat and huge aviator sunglasses. The only thing she could name for sure was his white skin color. The front license plate was smudged with something black after the first two alphanumeric characters.

The SUV bounced over the curb and tore off in the opposite direction as the semi. More horns blared as the driver cut off morning commuters and wove through traffic in its flight.

The trailer banged into the rear of Susan's rental car, ramming her head against the pillar. The vehicle spun until it faced the oncoming cars and kept turning until it was headed into the trailer's smoking and screeching rear tires.

What a stupid way to die. Susan tightened her grip on the steering wheel, closed her eyes, and waited to be crushed under the eighteen-wheeler.

Everything went silent except for her blood roaring in her ears. Her rental car stopped moving.

Then came a tapping at the driver-side window.

She swallowed hard and opened her eyes. A Hispanic man in black and white plaid flannel knocked on her window again.

"You okay, lady?" His voice was muffled.

She nodded and reached for the door handle. Luckily, the door opened. Adrenaline surged. She jumped out of the car and jogged to the back of the trailer despite what the motion did to her aching head.

But her assailant was long gone.

By the time, Susan and the semi-truck driver assured each other they were okay and exchanged insurance information, the Hermanville police, fire, and EMTs finally showed up.

Thankfully, there were multiple witnesses to the incident itself. Susan gave what little description of the driver she could. But the semi driver noticed the bruising and lump above her temple, and he insisted the EMTs check her out. In turn, the EMTs insisted she sit on the edge of their truck's bay so one of them could check her vitals while his partner examined the semi-driver on the curb.

"Your eyes are responding," the paramedic said flashing his damn little penlight right in her pupils. "That doesn't mean you don't have a concussion or a skull fracture."

"My sister and my cousins hit harder when I was a kid," she snapped. "If I survived them, I'll survive this."

He grimaced. "Fine, I'll back off, but I'm gonna to need you to sign a waiver that you refused transport to the hospital."

"Don't worry." She graced him with a smile to indicate there were no hard feelings. "I promise I won't sue you for my stupidity."

"All the accident victims say that." He chuckled. "Then their sister or their cousin, who happens to be an attorney, convinces them it's my fault for not forcing them to go to the hospital."

She leaned a little closer. "I'm that sister or cousin."

His eyebrows rose. "You're an attorney?"

"'Fraid so."

"I won't hold it against you." He grinned. "Sure I can't talk you into letting the hospital x-ray that skull of yours though?"

"If the headache gets worse or my vision goes fuzzy, I promise I'll call a rideshare and head straight to the ER." Susan crossed her heart.

One of the cops approached. "If you're not going to the ER, Ms. Kennedy, I have some more questions for you."

Crap. Maybe she should have gone to the dang hospital after all.

Chapter 8

The bad guys swept through the hostages and confiscated any phones, tablets, or other electronic devices anyone carried. Their leader, who Aisha silently nicknamed Alphahole, checked each phone number against the number for the Ghost Owl Aisha had entered on his burner phone.

Well, he was definitely thorough. Thank goodness, Tim and Arthur anticipated a contingency like this. Not only were Aisha and Rey's alter egos phone numbers routed through a series of fake numbers to their personal phones, so were the phone numbers of their firm's clients. It added a level of secret identity protection neither the government or other attorneys and agents could provide.

Judge Castillo sat next to his bailiff. Castillo had pulled off his robes to staunch the entrance and exit wounds of the downed man. The court reporter glared at Alphahole while the court recorder quietly sobbed beside the two men. Aisha, Carol, Jim, and the rookie prosecutor Jim was training sat nearby and leaned against the jury box.

The gunmen had the hostages in the gallery push the benches against the main doors to the courtroom to form a barricade. The civilians, attorneys, and prisoners huddled in the middle of the bare carpet with the guard who had been shot. A family member of a defendant was a nurse. He managed to form a tourniquet from the guard's belt and bandages from volunteered clothing.

"You need to take the lead negotiating with these people," Jim whispered in Aisha's ear.

"I don't have anything to use," she whispered back.

"He's interested in you and your client." Jim's hot breath tickled her ear and her nose. Despite the mints he'd eaten before court, she could still smell the onions and peppers from his breakfast burrito. "That gives you a leg up."

Alphahole sauntered over to them. "Care to share with the rest of the class why one of them is going to die, Ms. Franklin?"

"We were debating how much your people want to do life in prison for aggravated murder." She inclined her head toward the injured bailiff.

Alphahole stared at her for a long time. Aisha didn't flinch or avert her eyes.

Finally, he said, "Aren't you going to beg for his life? Or the other guard? Tell me I'd lessen the potential consequences by showing mercy?"

"You have no plans of letting any of us go."

"And what makes you think that?"

"If all you wanted was the Ghost Owl, you would have simply abducted me instead of taking an entire federal courtroom hostage." Aisha crossed her fingers she hadn't pushed him too far.

"I was told you were the smart one." From the crinkle of skin around Alphahole's eyes, he was grinning beneath the mask. "Little Miss Snake-in-the-Grass."

At the hated moniker, Jim inhaled sharply next to her. It had been bestowed on her by one of their classmates when she bested him in moot court.

She narrowed her eyes. "Guess it's a good thing I'm not a super. I doubt if you'd have the balls to say that to Cobblestone or Captain Mojave."

Alphahole chuckled. "Bet you wish you have superstrength right now. Or superspeed."

"Actually, I wish I had laser vision so I could cook you and your cronies," Aisha shot back.

"Oooo! Isn't that a little violent for someone who claims to represent superheroes?" He pointedly shifted his attention to Carol who lifted her chin.

"She's only here because her partner agreed to represent me," Carol said hotly.

"The same partner you kidnapped?"

Aisha watched the exchange. She recognized the tactic, had used it court and depositions many times herself. Now, why would Alphahole be trying to get the hostages wound up? What was he hoping they'd accidentally reveal? Did he think the Ghost Owl was in the courtroom?

Her blood chilled at the last thought. Alphahole didn't know for certain but he must suspect the superhero was here.

He crouched next to Carol. "Let's be honest with each other, Ms. Inunza. You helped Miss Purrfection escape from prison, which means you probably know some of her associates. I'll let you and the rest of the hostages go if you can tell me where the original Ghost Owl is."

Carol's face screwed into a thoroughly confused expression. "What are you talking about? The fake Captain Justice killed him in a battle over Lake Del Oro last summer. The videos of that night are all over the internet."

"You know the first rule of supers, Counselor." He stroked her cheek with the back of his gloved hand. "No body, no death."

Carol jerked away from him. "Miss Purrception never mentioned the Ghost Owl to me."

Alphahole grabbed the hair at the back of Carol's head and jerked her closer to him. She cried out.

"Stop it!" Aisha was on her knees before she realized she'd moved. A hard object poked her in the back, no doubt a gun barrel.

Alphahole stared at her. "Do you propose to give me the information that I want?"

She gulped air, but it stunk of the fear from the hostages. "You said you wanted the new Ghost Owl. You never said a thing about the original."

"That doesn't answer my question, Ms. Franklin."

"The original is dead," Aisha said.

Alphahole cocked his head. "Except the original met with Byron Trubble in front of your office a couple of days after his alleged death."

Aisha swallowed hard. She hated giving this jerk any information. He might be ex-Corvus for all she knew. But maybe a bit of truth would throw him off until she could come up with a better idea of how to disarm the bad guys and get the hostages out alive.

"That wasn't the original Ghost Owl," she said. "I was the person dressed as the Owl who met with Trubble that night."

CHAPTER 9

Harri rose from her office chair. "You can't go down to the federal courthouse half-cocked, Rey."

"The hostage situation is all over the news!" Rey stomped over to her desk.

Hard enough to rattle her equipment on the hardwood surface and slosh java over the edge of her mug.

"Who were you talking to?" he demanded.

"Eddie's new boss at the FBI." Harri circled her desk and gazed up at Rey. He was no longer the innocent kid who saved her from a three-story fall, and a lot of that change was her fault. "She doesn't want any supers on the scene, but we convinced her to let us send two."

Harri looked at Tim and Arthur. "Don't just stand there. Get your equipment and get your asses moving." She turned to Steve. "Get Molly and Kerry on the phone. Apprise them of the situation. They need to be at the courthouse in fourteen minutes. Tell Molly to bring Mitch down here on her way out. I'll watch him while she's busy."

Steve nodded and rose, but he hesitated beside Rey and looked at Harri. "We still need someone posing as the Ghost Owl. I should be the one who goes in."

Rey glared at his twin. "You said you didn't want to be a super-hero."

Steve pursed his lips, obviously trying to control his own temper. "I would be the decoy, not the hero."

"If you think you can just waltz in and take my place—"

"If you go in, your focus will be on your wife, not the other hostages," Steve bit out. "Aisha's keeping her head low and stalling for a reason."

"Or I could go in as the Ghost Owl," Harri mused.

"No!" they both said at the same time. The twins looked at her with matching aggravated expressions. Well, except Rey had a beard and Steve didn't.

Tim poked his head around the door frame. "Why do you all want to be me? And none of you ask. Aisha had the grace to ask."

"The bad guys want you, sweetie," Harri growled. "And whoever *they* are wants you dead."

"Maybe it's time to draw *them* out." Tim scowled right back at her.

"You promised," she hissed. They'd fought about him retiring from the supers game, and it took a mind-controlled Steve nearly killing Tim for reality to sink in. He'd be fifty next year, he wasn't a super, and he'd broken his body over the decades as the vigilante known as the Ghost Owl.

Tim's right jaw muscle twitched, an indication she had crossed a line. She didn't care what the twins thought. They weren't the ones who sat by Tim's bedside through three surgeries.

And they were looking at a right knee replacement now that his left leg was as healed as it was going to be.

"You'll be on site, Tim," Steve said. "You can guide me through the comms."

"You're not going—" Rey started heatedly.

"I'm the fake Ghost Owl." A wry smile crossed Steve's face. "A decoy. The real Ghost Owl is going to need Black Falcon to bring her the right outfit for the occasion. And regardless of what Special Agent in Charge Consuelo thinks, the girls are going to need back-up."

"'The girls are going to need backup'?" Harri spat.

"Molly and Kerry are only a couple of years older than us," Rey said with a smirk. "And you've been 'mommying' me since we met. So, yeah. Girls."

"That's ageist," Harri sputtered.

"Hey, I'd feel better about Sparx going instead of the two of us." Steve waved his hand between himself and Rey. "But she needs to be with her mom at the doctor's evaluation today."

Harri hated to admit it, but she would have felt better if Steve's girlfriend Qiang Reilly, AKA the superhero Sparx, was available, too. Sometimes, she even wondered if the bad guys had a contract with Fate herself. Things always seemed to go wrong at the worst possible time.

"I can keep the boys from squabbling." Tim grinned.

The twins both looked at her with the same eyebrows-raised expression, questioning whether she'd point out Tim's obvious dig.

"Fine." She raised her hands in surrender. "But if you *boys* get anyone killed, you'll need a proctologist to get my shoes out of your asses. And that includes you, Canyon."

"Yes, ma'am," the three men chorused. They trooped out of her office.

After the building's antique elevator rumbled into gear to take the guys to their respective floors, Patty poked her head around the doorjamb. "Everything okay?"

Harri rested her left hip on the corner of her desk. "I don't like any of them walking into danger, but with the weirdness of the last couple of months, I wonder if this is a trap."

"Of course it is," Patty asserted.

"Have you developed superpowers now? You can see the future?"

"No." Patty grinned. "It's just been how our luck's been running for the last year and a half."

CHAPTER 10

"You should have gunned the engine when he rammed you instead of braking," Jeff, one of the baristas, offered. "Any SUV outweighs a compact sedan like yours by a couple of thousand pounds." He and the café's manager stood next to the table where Susan was being questioned by one of Hermanville's finest.

She glared up at the kid, but she couldn't get too lippy. He had brought her ice in a towel for her head. Plus, she needed the cop questioning her on her side.

"My partner noticed none of the airbags deployed," the officer noted.

"There's no side airbags in that model," Jeff said. "The semi spun her like a top, but she was never hit head-on."

The officer's jaw worked a couple of times before he said, "Thank you for your help."

Susan stifled a laugh. Good to know the barista wasn't irritating only her.

The officer jotted down the information and turned his attention back to Susan. "Did you happen to get the license plate number?"

"Only an 'M' and a '1' or an 'I'. The rest of the front plate was blacked out. Sorry."

"If he was so close to you, how'd you see the front plate?" the cop said.

"Like Jeff said, the accident spun my rental around." Susan set the makeshift ice pack on the table and looked up at the manager. "Did anyone in here see the rear of the SUV?"

The manager shook her head. "Sally at the window saw you being pushed, and Jeff caught the rest because he was emptying the trash." She crossed her arms and frowned. "Our security camera may have caught it if they didn't obscure the back plate, too,"

The cop nodded "Let's take a look."

"Jeff, would you replace Ms. Kennedy's order?" the manager said before she turned back to Susan. "Sorry, but we had to throw your drinks and cream cheese out because it's been too long since they were at serving temperature. Food safety rules."

The kid tried to look pleasant as his manager strode toward the café office with the cop in tow. "I'll be right back with your replacement order." He bobbed his head and headed for the counter.

"Don't forget the cream cheese," Susan called after him. She pulled out her phone and thumbed her client's personal number.

"Hello?"

"Hey, Eugenia! It's Susan Kennedy."

Part of addressing Mother Defiant by her given name was so no one in the café would know who Susan was talking to. The other part enjoyed the superhero's discomfiture over the Catholic saint she was named after.

"Is everything okay?" Eugenia said.

"I'm going to be late." Susan grimaced as the tow truck operator finished loading what was left of her rental car. She was damn lucky to be alive. "An idiot rear-ended me in the drive-thru as I was picking up our breakfast."

There was a sharp gasp. "Are you okay?"

"Yes, I'm fine." Susan watched the tow truck with her rental pull out into traffic. The poor semi driver was still waiting for a repair truck that specialized in eighteen-wheelers. His front fender had been shoved into the first right tire. It seemed to be the only damage to his rig other than some scratches on the rear of the trailer. Three other officers were directing traffic around the disabled semi. "I'm just waiting for my replacement vehicle. It should be here in ten to fifteen minutes."

"All right." Eugenia exhaled. "Are you sure you're up to this?"

"Dewey isn't going to give either of us a time-out," Susan said sourly.

"Are you sure he wasn't behind your accident?" Eugenia said.

Susan tapped the fingers of her right hand on her laptop case. The suspicion had also crossed her mind. "I don't know." She sighed. "But I wouldn't put it past him."

Despite everything, Susan made it to Eugenia's condo by nine a.m. The superhero answered her door in a pale pink t-shirt, gray yoga pants, and her dark hair pulled into a messy bun. In other words, she looked like every other suburban housewife.

"Holy crap! You are going to have one heck of a shiner tomorrow." But she held the door open for Susan to enter. A male someone was talking rather loudly further in the condo.

"Is that Jared?" Susan asked.

"Yeah, he's on the phone with Harri about the hostage situation." Eugenia took the cup carrier from Susan and beckoned her to follow.

"What hostage situation?"

Eugenia frowned as they entered the kitchen. "The hostage situation at the federal courthouse in Canyon Pointe. It's been all over the news this morning."

A counter separated the kitchen from the family room where Jared Krasowski, AKA Blue Racer and also Eugenia's significant other, paced in front of the fireplace while he talked on the phone. At least, he wasn't moving fast enough to set the carpet on fire.

Their large screen TV hung over the fireplace. The picture showed one of the Action 12! News reporters standing in Founder's Green with a serious crisis expression on his face and a police barricade behind him. The sound was muted while Jared talked on the phone.

Susan's heart pounded harder than it did when she thought she was going to be ground chuck under the semi. Aisha had taken Carol's arraignment hearing so Susan could fly up to Hermanville. "I've spent the morning talking to the police, my insurance company, and the car rental office."

"Oh, crap! I'm sorry, Susan." Eugenia appeared truly contrite. "I wasn't thinking." Her lack of understanding of emotional and social cues was worse than Arthur Drallhickey's, but she meant well.

At their conversation, Jared turned and strode toward the counter. "She just arrived." He held out his phone to Susan. "Harri wants to talk to you."

Susan accepted the portable device and held it to her ear. "What the hell is happening down there?" She listened as her partner filled her in, including the fact Judge Castillo's court was the one with the hostages.

"Do you need us down there?" Susan asked. "I can book the next flight—"

"The new head of the FBI office here is being a pain in the ass about any supers helping." From Harri's disgusted tone, someone at the firm was about to do something stupid, and Susan didn't have to guess who or why.

She glanced at Jared and Eugenia who were hanging on every word. "Please tell me this isn't about the original Ghost Owl again."

"Yep." Harri paused before she asked, "How are you doing? Jared told me about your so-called accident."

Another chill ran through Susan. "They've made runs at Aisha and me today, so you need to be watching your back."

"Patty and I already got that lecture from the guys, thank you." For all of Harri's normal grumpiness, worry lay beneath her tone. "We aren't leaving the Lechuza Building."

"We'll keep Susan safe," Eugenia yelled.

"I appreciate that, but—" Susan started.

"No arguments." Jared made a slashing motion with his hand that sent the paper napkins on the counter ruffling. "If someone's taking potshots at our attorneys, we're protecting the one here."

Harri laughed.

"I take it you heard that," Susan said dryly.

"Sleeping on their couch while you work on Mother Defiant's case isn't a bad idea," Harri said.

"Give Jared your keycard," Eugenia demanded. "He can get in and out with your belongings without anyone seeing him."

"All right, all right." Susan rolled her eyes, which didn't help her lingering headache.

"By the way, turn your ringer back on," Harri said. "I know you were dealing with the accident, but I did leave you a voicemail and a text."

"Yes, Mom." Susan rolled her eyes. Having two godchildren had brought out Harri's maternal instincts in full force, and she didn't know when to curb them.

Susan ended the call and handed Jared's phone back to him. "Thanks."

He stuck the phone in his jeans pocket, held out his hand, and waggled his fingers. "Key card."

She reluctantly handed over the black plastic rectangle with the name of the hotel stenciled in white. "I still need to check out."

"I'll take care of it." He grinned before he disappeared. The ruffled paper napkins and the waving fronds of the decorative fern in the family room were the only evidence of his presence.

Eugenia's mouth twisted into a wry half-grimace, half-smile. "I hope he remembers to change into his Blue Racer outfit. His super-speed is hell on denim."

CHAPTER 11

Aisha held her breath. If Alphahole tried to kill Carol, she would have to stop him, and her secret would be out. Or the minion behind her would shoot, and her secret would still be out.

"Now, why on earth would you be trying to fool Trubble?" Alphahole finally said.

"We needed some information." Aisha stared him in the eyes. "Trubble would only deal with the original Ghost Owl. The general knew damn well the Ghost Owl would give it to us. I just cut out the middleman."

"How did you trick Trubble into believing you were the original?" He was paying attention to her, and he released Carol. She sat up straighter and rubbed her head where he yanked on her hair.

Aisha shrugged. "A couple of years ago, Frentic Costumes put out a kids' version of his costume based on the only clear photograph of the original Ghost Owl. With my contacts, I had an adult-sized replica made for a Halloween party. With a few electronic tricks and my custom outfit, he bought I was the original."

"Trubble isn't that stupid." Alphahole's attention darted around the well. Was he considering who to shoot next?

Everything coalesced in Aisha's mind, the who and the why. "What is Corvus's obsession with the original Ghost Owl?"

"How should I know?" he sneered.

"Because you're ex-Corvus."

Alphahole laughed. "Why would I be one of those losers?"

"Your boss was in prison. Maybe you miss him?"

"Your client helped his escape," Alphahole shot back before he glanced at Carol. "Seems to be a theme here."

"But the original Ghost Owl made arrangements to deliver all the evidence he collected on Corvus to the authorities." Aisha shrugged again. "He took Corvus down, and you want revenge on a dead man."

No one in the courtroom said anything. Aisha waited. Had she pushed Alphahole too far?

Aisha's phone rang with the Meredith Brooks' "Bitch". Both Aisha and Jeremy kept that ring tone for Harri's cell.

Alphahole pulled Aisha's phone out of one of the equipment pockets of his tactical pants and touched the screen a couple of times. "You'd better have what I want Winters. Or I'll use your partner's brains to practice my expressionist skills."

"The current Ghost Owl is on his way to the courthouse." Harri's voice came clearly through the speaker. "He'll turn himself over to you in return for releasing the hostages."

"No." The skin around Alphahole's eyes crinkled again. "He'll come up here to Judge Castillo's courtroom. And I'll let the hostages go if I'm satisfied he's the real thing."

"Have you met the new head of the FBI office here in Canyon Pointe?" Harri sighed. "She's looking to make a name for herself. You and your people will be collateral damage in her rise to power. Ghost Owl can get your people out of the courthouse alive."

"If we die, do you really think the hostages will still be alive?" Alphahole sneered.

"I don't think Special Agent in Charge Consuelo gives a shit about them either." Harri sounded very tired. How much arguing had been happening at their office this morning? Was the hostage situation on the news already? Was Harri struggling to keep Rey and Tim from enacting some stupid plan?

"Let me guess, you're the only one who cares about the precious innocents." He laughed. "Though the fellow attorney you're representing is just as guilty as I am."

"Is that the issue?" Harri said dryly. "You couldn't afford an attorney, and you're pissed the public defender couldn't get you off?"

"If that's the level of your wit, Carol Inunza is screwed."

"Tell her the truth," Aisha bit out. When Alphahole said nothing, Aisha said, "He's a crow, Harri."

"I never said that," Alphahole said.

Aisha could feel him smirking beneath the mask.

"Ah, but you just did." Harri's throaty laugh echoed out of the speaker. "Damn. Is that what this is all about? Killing a bunch of innocent people because we pissed off your disgraced boss?"

Aisha could feel Jim, Carol, and Judge Castillo's attention on her, but she focused on Alphahole. The jab of the gun barrel in her back disappeared.

"What are they talking about?" a male voice growled from above her.

"The ladies are just trying to get under our skin. Thank you for the information, Ms. Winters." Alphahole ended the call and gestured at Aisha with her phone. "I suggest you sit down, Ms. Franklin. If you really want to save these people, that is."

She slowly sat down next to Carol.

"Boss," one of the minions near the main doors called out. "The FBI say they have the Ghost Owl. We need to release the injured people before they will allow him to come in."

Blood roared in Aisha's ears. Who the hell would be stupid enough to dress as her alter ego? Her stomach sank. Nearly everyone at the Lechuza Building.

And her husband topped the list.

CHAPTER 12

Harri wanted to throw her own smart phone across the room. Instead, she closed her eyes and took a deep breath. "Did you guys catch all that?"

"Yeah," Tim said over the comm in her right ear. "This is a lot of trouble and effort to go through to kill the original Ghost Owl."

"There's more." She related her conversations with Blue Racer and Susan.

"Divide and conquer," Tim murmured.

"No shit, Sherlock," Harri snapped. "And no, I'm not leaving the Lechuza Building."

"I was going to say maybe you could call Rue Liberty."

Suspicion sparked in her brain. "You've already called her, haven't you?"

The comm crackled and a feminine voice said, "No, I did."

"Molly!"

"Suck it up, Harri." Molly Reinhold, AKA Nix, didn't sound like her usual bubbly self. "We can't leave you, Patty, and the kids alone. Not if the remnants of Corvus are on the warpath again."

The intercom buzzed. Too much was happening this morning, and she'd barely touched her to-do list.

"I've got to go. Comms off for now." Harri pulled the comm out of her ear and set the device in its case and closed the lid. Comms and attorney-client privilege did not mix. The intercom buzzed again.

She repressed a groan and tapped the appropriate button. "Yeah, Patty?"

"It's Nella. She wants a statement." Of course, she did. Nella Lopez was the news producer at Action 12!

Harri groaned. Aisha normally handled the media duties. Maybe Harri should have taken care of the arraignment after all. Terrorists were easier to deal with than reporters.

"Put her through."

The light for line 1 started blinking on Harri's phone set. She reluctantly picked up the receiver and pressed the button. "Harri Winters."

"I know you don't like me, but Aisha is kind of indisposed, and I need a statement," Nella said in a rush.

"There's a reason she's indisposed," Harri said. "And I like you just fine. You know there's only one person I hate at your station. But let's face the truth. My partner gives you better sound bites than I do. Not to mention, the new head of our city's FBI office is refusing to cooperate with Ted."

Nella chuckled. "Well, that last part is true. He called her a 'little lady', and she threatened to arrest him for obstruction this morning."

"If you could set up a cage match between the two of them, you could make millions," Harri suggested. That made Nella laugh even harder.

"Winters and Franklin's official position is that we're doing everything we can to cooperate with the authorities," Harri said.

Nella's humor died. "How are you doing personally?"

"I'm scared," Harri admitted. "This can end very badly if everyone's not careful."

"If I send Essie to your office, would you be willing to do a quick live statement for the early evening news?" Nella asked. "She'll send you a copy of potential questions this afternoon, but you need to realize—"

"Circumstances could change in the next few hours, so all bets are off." Harri sighed. "As long as it's Essie, I agree." Essie Morales was one of the evening news anchors at Action 12! Even better, she wasn't a total jerk like her co-anchor Ted Meadowfield.

"Thanks, Harri. Essie and the truck will be there by five to set up." Nella hung up.

Harri set the receiver back in its cradle. She reached for her coffee, but the mug was cold.

Of course, it was. She'd poured her morning caffeine around seven-forty-five this morning. The little clock on her laptop screen said it was already half past ten. She forgotten to turn on Tim's warming coaster invention, which was probably best after Rey's stomping sloshed java all over the device. And if she focused on the mess and the cold coffee, she wouldn't totally lose it over Aisha and Carol being trapped with a bunch of crazies.

She opened the bottom drawer on her desk and grabbed some spare napkins to clean up the coffee that had sloshed all over the coaster. Once she wiped up the coffee, made sure her coaster worked, and checked that Mitch was still asleep in his infant carrier, she stood and headed for the break room with the cool mug.

Patty looked up as Harri approached her desk. "Any news?"

Harri shook her head. "Not yet. Essie Morales will be here later this afternoon to do a live broadcast for the evening news."

"You agreed to that?" Patty wore a quizzical expression.

Harri couldn't blame their assistant. Her aversion to the press went back to when they both worked at City Hall.

"I'm the only partner available." Harri shrugged. "And Carol's arraignment was an expected news item."

"Which was the real reason Aisha was at the courthouse, not you." Patty smirked.

"But I'd be one of the casualties." Harri grimaced. "She's going to feel guilty as hell if anyone dies."

"Crap." Patty made a face. "Her secret identity could be totally blown, too."

"Yeah." Harri stared at her cup a moment. "You want some coffee now that you can drink it." The perky blonde had finally weaned her daughter. As a result, she tackled caffeine and alcohol with equal gusto.

"No, thanks." Patty smiled. "But I wouldn't mind a cola."

"Diet or high octane?"

"High octane. It's going to be a long day."

Harri took one step toward the before pounding came from the front doors.

Both woman looked toward the entrance. Outside, Judge Pablo Inunza raised his fist and banged on the bullet-proof glass again.

"Yep, definitely a long day," Patty muttered.

Chapter 13

◆━━━━━●◆●━━━━━◆

Susan was explaining to Eugenia her motion for summary judgment and what would happen if the judge didn't grant it when Blue Racer entered the family room with her suitcase.

"I'm really sorry." He set down the little apple green hard shell and pushed back his cowl. "Someone ransacked your hotel room."

Susan grimaced. "How bad?"

"Your cosmetics were a total loss. I won't repeat what they wrote on the bathroom mirror with the mascara." He gestured at the suitcase. "Some of your clothes were destroyed, but I packed everything. You can decide what you want to keep, and we'll wash those for you."

"Before we do anything, let me check what you brought back here." Susan rose and pulled out her phone. She didn't relish any client seeing her unmentionables, but these were extenuating circumstances. She activated Tim's special app, popped open the hard shell, and scanned the suitcase and contents.

"Now, that's a useful app," Eugenia murmured from behind her.

The indicator remained green, indicating the app couldn't detect any bugs. Susan turned it off and slipped it back into her pocket. None of this made any sense. Why did they search her room if they planned to kill her? And what were they looking for?

"By the way, I reported the break-in to the hotel manager." Jared scowled. "The guy was a dick, but I got him to issue a credit."

Susan blinked. "That wasn't necessary."

"It was the right thing to do," Jared insisted.

"Honey, go change into your civvies before the Kravitts decide to check on us again," Eugenia said with an amused expression.

He zipped out of the family room, and the rush of air from his departure at superspeed blew papers around the room.

Eugenia sighed. "I'm sorry about that. He forgets he's living with someone sometimes." She knelt and collected the sheets from the carpet.

"There has to be pluses about living with him," Susan said as she reordered the scattered paperwork as Eugenia handed it to her.

A sweet smiled filled Eugenia's face. "He's the first guy I've ever dated who could handle my powers. Especially the truth-telling part."

"What do you mean?"

"I didn't have a whole lot of control over my powers when I was a teenager. Guys only want to get in your pants at that age." A self-deprecating laugh burbled from Eugenia. "It didn't help when they'd confess their desires in front of my dad."

"Ouch," Susan said. "I'm surprised your parents would even let you date with those kind of confessions."

"It got to the point where no one wanted to be around me." Eugenia shrugged. "And I really didn't want to be around them. It seemed like no one liked me for me. They all wanted something."

"I never thought about it from that standpoint." Susan clipped the papers together and set the bundle on the open folder. "Is that why you keep people at arm's length?"

"Yeah." Eugenia hugged herself. "I know I have a reputation as a bitch, but I just get so angry—"

"So why do you trust me?"

"You were honest about how much money you could make me from the start."

"And Dewey and Cheatham?" Susan prompted.

"Howard Dewey really believed he could promote my licensing to the next level." Eugenia stared out the sliding glass windows that showed the tiny patio and its high fence. "I didn't ask him the right questions." She turned her attention back to Susan. "And I really apologize for not listening to you. You're the only one besides Jared I feel comfortable with."

Susan crossed her arms. She didn't really want to know, but the information may have a bearing on what was happening now, both the attempt on her life and Aisha being taken hostage since they'd both worked for Howard Dewey at one time.

"Eugenia, I need to ask you a couple of questions, and I really need you to be honest with me. When did Dewey first contact you, and what did he say to you about me or Aisha Franklin?"

The superhero's cheeks flushed bright pink. "It was all bullshit. I know that now. Can we just forget about it?"

Susan dropped her arms to her sides. "I'm not blaming you for everything that happened. Obviously, I failed to build sufficient trust between us, even with taking one of your powers into account. But I need to know what they said because I think it may have something to do with the hostage situation in Canyon Pointe and the attempt on my life today."

Eugenia gulped air, and she started to tremble. "At the beginning, he said you were ungrateful for the opportunities he gave you. That you were greedy, and you were probably giving me false statements about my income." Tears welled in her eyes. "He thought he was telling the truth because that's exactly what he did so he expected other attorneys like you to do the same."

She swallowed hard before she could continue. "Then I saw he was nickel-and-diming every little thing, and he wasn't even doing the work! It was some junior attorney fresh out of law school. Howard wouldn't even take my calls." She shrugged. "That's when I talked with Jared about what was happening, and asked him how he felt about his lawyer."

"And I said I loved Harri and Aisha." Jared entered the family room, crossed to where Eugenia stood, and wrapped his left arm around her waist. He looked at Susan. "And I told her you had joined Winters and Franklin."

"I went to Dewey and Cheatham one last time and asked to talk to Howard." Eugenia swiped at the wetness on her cheeks. "When I got the brush-off I expected, I gave the junior attorney a copy of the termination letter, told her I was firing Dewey and Cheatham as my representation, and left."

"Let me guess," Susan said dryly. "Howard caught you before you left the building."

"Before I even got on the elevator," Eugenia said with a rueful expression. "First, he gave me the 'you'll never work in this town again' speech. Then it turned into an attack—" Breath hissed between her teeth.

"I'm a big girl," Susan said. "And Howard Dewey's favorite word for a woman who has crossed him is 'cunt.'"

Eugenia nodded. "Yeah, it is. Then he really melted down about how Aisha had ruined a multi-billion dollar real estate deal and lost him a lot of money and how much he hated her for it. That if I signed with Winters and Franklin, he would make me regret it."

"Wait a minute." Susan waved her hands. "Did Howard say what property it was he lost money on?"

Eugenia shook her shook morosely. "He was still cursing a storm when he stomped back down the hallway towards his law office. It was almost like he forgot I was there. I dropped off the certified original in the mail on the way back to Jared's apartment."

Holy crap. What if today's incidents had nothing to do directly with Corvus? And everything to do with a bunch of rich white guys trying to take over the Canyon Block? The same guys who helped Corvus set up Tim Canyon for the murder of his wife and son twenty-one years ago?

Susan's heart hammered even harder. This could be the link between Dewey and Cheatham, a group of disgraced politicians, and Corvus Harri had been searching for.

CHAPTER 14

Anxiety assailed Aisha while Alphahole stared at her. Finally, he said, "You cooperated so you get your wish, Ms. Franklin. Rojo, Amarillo, grab a couple of the jury chairs and take the two injured men down to the first floor."

So their assailants were code-named with colors in Spanish. It was her first bit of information about who or what she may be dealing with since they invaded the courtroom. Too bad she didn't have a clue of what it meant.

The jury chairs were on wheels. It wasn't a perfect method of transportation, but hopefully, it would keep the two men alive until they reached the paramedics outside the building.

If only she could find a way to get rid of a couple more of the minions, she might have a chance against Alphahole and his freaks. It would mean blowing her secret identity after all the hard work she and Susan had done to ramp up the Ghost Owl brand, but her superhero career wasn't worth these people's lives.

While Alphahole directed the movement of the two injured men, Aisha leaned closer to Jim. "How well do you know the back hallways on this floor?"

"Good enough," he whispered back. "But even if we can get the hostages away from the ones in here, these jerks will have someone watching the stairwells."

"There's a taser in my purse," she barely breathed the words. "How good of a shot are you?"

"Don't you know how to work it?" Jim looked at her askance.

"I'll be taking care of the rest of the bad guys."

Jim started to laugh, but he turned it into a cough when Alphahole looked at him while his minions loaded the bailiff onto the wheeled chair. Even Judge Castillo gave them a funny expression.

"Have you been doing too much work with supers?" Jim hissed once the minions rolled the bailiff away.

"Do you trust me?"

"With my life?"

She glanced at Jim and nodded.

He sucked in a deep breath and slowly released it before his chin dipped once.

Alphahole marched back into the well and eyed them. "What's more interesting to you than surviving?"

"I just reminded Mr. Duncan he still owes me two hundred dollars from a poker game," Aisha said coolly.

"You don't strike me as the poker type, Ms. Franklin." Alphahole pointed his handgun at her. "Care to try again?"

"Man, she was trying to lighten the mood." Jim looked at the hostages in the gallery before his attention returned to Alphahole. "You might want to organize these people and take them to the restrooms in small groups before the FBI cuts off the utilities to the building. Else it's going to get very smelly in here really fast."

Alphahole stared at Jim for a long time before he said, "Verde,

Morado, you two are on bathroom detail." He waved his gun at the people in the well. "Take the four women here first."

The court clerk and the court reporter shakily got to their feet. Aisha stood and helped Carol upright since her wrists and ankles were still chained together.

"Any of them get lippy, shoot them," Alphahole ordered.

"Yes, sir," they both answered in clipped tones.

Aisha led the way toward the main doors of the courtroom, her right hand wrapped around Carol's left elbow to keep her upright while her client took short, mincing steps. In her brainstorming, she'd forgotten about the prisoners' ankle cuffs. It would be a bitch to get the accused out unless some of the other hostages dragged them along. Doing so would slow everyone down unless one of the other guards had a key with them.

Or unless Aisha broke the chains. Yet, another way to blow her secret identity to the heavens.

Unfortunately, the public bathrooms were three courtrooms down from Judge Castillo's courtroom, around the corner of the hallway, and past the elevators. It took their little group nearly five minutes to reach them.

The guards followed the women inside the restroom. Thankfully, the two minions assigned to watch them didn't insist on the ladies leaving the door open. Aisha went with Carol into the handicap stall to help her with her clothes. Thank goodness, she had a two-piece inmate outfit. If she had been wearing a jumpsuit, it would have been next to impossible to get it to where she could use the toilet with the cuffs on her wrists.

Also, the guards didn't say a peep while their little group washed their hands. It may mean nothing in the long run, but Aisha wanted to be a good example to Mitch.

They exited the restroom as the elevator doors slid open. Two minions stepped out, or they could be the same two who took the injured men downstairs. They motioned for someone else to exit.

The Ghost Owl stepped out of the car. Except this person had six inches on her with her heels on. But the detail on their outfit was exactly like hers. She'd recognize Jeremy's careful stitching any-where.

The Ghost Owl inclined their head. "A pleasure to see you again, Ms. Franklin. Or should I say Jatz'om Kuh?"

CHAPTER 15

Harri set her cup of cold coffee on the raised lip of Patty's desk and turned to her. "Buzz him in."

Their assistant looked up at her while the judge pounded on the glass for a third time. "You sure that's a good idea with everything going on this morning?"

She had a point. Inunza's grandfather was a super, and they only had Inunza's word that the judge himself had no powers. Not to mention Mitch was sleeping in Harri's office.

"Where's Frisco?"

"Downstairs in the computer lab," Patty answered. "Arthur has him practicing coding. Javier is upstairs with Grace."

"Get Mitch and Frisco upstairs. I'll take care of this," Harri murmured.

A fierce look filled Patty's face as she rose and jogged for Harri's office. Patty and the older kids knew how to operate the security measures. They'd shut down the elevator and lock the stairwell doors once they were all ensconced in the panic room in the Esperanzas' apartment.

Harri leaned over Patty's desk and pressed the button for the front door's intercom. "With all due respect, Your Honor, what do you want?"

"Have you seen the news?" he demanded.

"Yes, and I've been in touch with the FBI about what's happening at the federal courthouse. However, that doesn't answer my question."

His dark brown eyes burned through the glass and into her heart. "What are you doing to save my wife? Or is this whole hostage situation how you're really getting back at her for kidnapping you?"

From the corner of Harri's eye, she caught Patty trotting for the elevator with the infant carrier in her hands. "Actually, we believe my partners are the real targets."

Confusion spread across his face. "Why would someone target Susan Kennedy at the courthouse?"

Harri frowned as she realized a couple of things were wrong. "Why weren't you at Carol's arraignment this morning to support her?"

Inunza slumped against the glass. "She didn't want me there. And I can't find Paul."

Worry tried to choke the words in Harri's throat. "What do you mean you can't find Paul?"

"Carol didn't want either of us at her arraignment, in case she wasn't granted bail," Inunza said. "Paul's been working at Mesquite Pool for the last couple of years. He said he was scheduled to work this morning, but his supervisor phoned the house and asked if he could come in for another lifeguard who called in sick. She said Paul wasn't answering his cell."

Crap. Paul was a good kid. Responsible. The judge was probably right in his unspoken fear that Paul had gone to the federal courthouse to support his mother despite Carol's wishes.

Her smart phone buzzed in her pocket with two short vibrations. Patty had locked down the upper floors. And both she and Javier had their own version of Tim's electroshock weapons that could take down most supers as well as regular bad guys.

"Come on in, Judge." Harri hit the control to unlock both sets of doors at the building's main entrance. The scanners between the two sets of glass didn't detect any weapons or listening devices.

Still, Inunza cautiously entered the foyer and approached the receptionist's desk, peering around. "Where'd your assistant go?"

Harri crossed her arms. "Judge, I've got kids in this building. One of my partners has been taken hostage at the federal courthouse, and someone tried to kill my other partner at a coffee shop drive-thru around the same time. I've got super clients at the courthouse. I've got super clients guarding Susan. And I've got more clients on their way here."

Inunza grimaced. "I apologize. I guess I was so wrapped up in my own problems I didn't stop to think you had your own."

She smiled at him. "I was about to get some coffee. Would you like a cup? Then we can talk."

"I . . ." He nodded. "Yes, thank you. I'd appreciate the coffee and the chat."

She picked up her mug of cold brew, and the intercom to the garage door crackled to life.

"Patty? It's Rue Liberty. I've got Cobblestone with me. Nix asked us to stop by."

Despite Molly calling her grandmother to babysit the Lechuza Building occupants, Harri appreciated the backup. She circled Patty's desk and pressed the response button. She was too damn short to keep reaching over the ledge. She'd tear a ligament at her age despite her regular workouts in Tim's gym downstairs.

"Hey, Rue! It's Harri. One second." She hit the lock for the garage door entrance.

Rue Liberty hobbled into the reception area with her cane. She was dressed in civilian clothes. Technically retired, she still showed the spunk from her days in the Forties, Fifties, and Sixties as a superhero. As usual, her silver hair was pulled back in a tidy bun, and her blue eyes sparkled behind her wire-rim frames.

Cobblestone followed, treading carefully so as not to break the antique Art Deco floor tiles. He, on the other hand, wore the forest green trunks that made up his superhero costume. With his pebbled, nearly impenetrable hide, all he needed was to be decent in public.

"Where's Patty?" Rue frowned and looked around.

"She's guarding the kids," Harri replied. "Let me warn her, and she'll unlock the elevator for you." She pulled the phone from her pocket and texted Patty the code word and the message.

There was a deep thunk from the center of the building. Then came the grumble and whine as the car slowly descended to the first floor.

"Can I bum a bottle of cola from you, Harri?" Cobblestone's deep bass rumbled. "I was up most of the night helping the fire department with a three alarm at an apartment building. In fact, I was just getting out of the shower when Rue called me."

"Sure. What's your poison, Rue?" Harri asked.

The elderly woman waved her free hand. "Nothing for me. Thank you though." She tottered toward the elevator.

Harri led the way to the breakroom. She retrieved the giant bottle of soda for the superhero out of the refrigerator and dumped her cold coffee before pouring herself and the judge fresh cups.

"Cobblestone, there's kolaches and bagels in the conference room if you're hungry." Harri gestured toward the door.

"No, thanks." He grinned. Well, as much as he could with his stiff, impenetrable skin. "I'll hang out on a couch in your foyer and read." He lumbered toward the right couch near the second set of doors.

Harri bit her tongue to keep from saying something rude. Cobblestone was doing her a favor. But with summer break still in full swing, the neighborhood kids would certainly spot the superhero, and there would be a crowd in front of the law office entrance by lunchtime.

Inunza followed Harri into her office. She shut the door for some privacy and crossed the room to the couches and coffee table by the huge front window. She hadn't even had a chance to raise the blinds this morning. She reached for the cord.

"Leave the blinds down, Harri."

She looked over her shoulder, and the cord slipped from her nerveless fingers. Inunza had what appeared to be a gun in his right hand, but it was bright red and looked like a children's toy. Tim and Arthur had started working in their new scanning device after 3-D printing for guns had become available. Even Arthur admitted it was foolish to think the government could stop anyone from using 3-D printing to create weapons.

Harri swallowed hard and met Inunza's eyes. "What's going on, Pablo?"

"I wasn't lying when I said Paul was missing." The gun trembled along with his hand. "I received a call. The same people who took over Castillo's courtroom also kidnapped my son. They sent this gun to me and said if I didn't kill you, Carol and Paul would be executed."

CHAPTER 16

Susan pulled out her phone and hit the speed dial for Harri's smart phone. It rang four times before rolling over to voicemail. She muttered a few choice words herself as she dialed the law firm's main number.

"Winters and Franklin. How may I assist you?" Patty chirped. However, Susan could hear babies and kids in the background.

"Patty? It's Susan."

"Oh, sorry," their assistant murmured. "There's a bug in the software that forwards the firm phones to my smart phone. It won't show the caller ID."

"I tried to call Harri's personal cell, but she's not picking up. Please tell me she didn't leave the Lechuza Building."

"No, she didn't," Patty assured Susan. "Judge Inunza showed up on our doorstep a few minutes ago, pretty upset too since his wife is one of the federal courthouse hostages. She's probably talking to him in her office."

An ugly suspicion filled Susan's gut. It wouldn't be the first time Howard Dewey had blackmailed a judge. She simply didn't have the proof for the first instance she learned about.

"Is there any super nearby you can call for backup?" she asked.

"Rue Liberty and Cobblestone just arrived." Patty giggled. "It almost caused a fight between Mom and Dad until Nix admitted she was the one who called Rue. She's up here with me and Cobblestone is downstairs with Harri."

"Give me his number, please."

"You think something's going on?"

"I hope not," Susan said. "But after the morning we've had, I'm not taking any chances."

Patty rattled off the number, and Susan scribbled it on her notepad. "Thanks, Patty. You and Rue keep the kids safe."

"You want me to head to Canyon Pointe?" Jared asked. "I can change."

"Not yet." Susan's thumbs tapped the digits into her phone.

It rang twice before a deep bass voice rumbled, "Hey, Ms. Kennedy. What's up?"

"Cobblestone, I need you to check on Harri right now."

"I can't do that. She's in her office with Judge Inunza. He's pretty shaken up about his wife."

"Look, you can blame it on me, but please check on her," Susan begged.

"All right," he said, sounding terribly unsure. "You wanna stay on the line?"

"Yes." She crossed the fingers of her right hand as the superhero's heavy footsteps echoed in the foyer and back through the phone receiver.

"Hey, Harri—" Cobblestone started to say.

Then came the sound of a gunshot.

CHAPTER 17

Jatz'om Kuh. The Mayan name of the Ghost Owl. The name everyone in the Canyon Block had known Tim by, and now her.

Aisha blinked. The helmet deliberately distorted the voice, but the tone, the inflection, the cadence were definitely Steve's. She nodded once. They flew into action at superspeed. In less than a second, they'd incapacitated the four minions and lowered them quietly to the floor.

"Black Falcon, I've made contact," Steve said. Did he realize the external speaker was on, or was this he way of reassuring her that he and Rey were working together?

Aisha breathed deeply. The situation looked a little brighter. "We need to hide these guys."

"Ladies, is there a back room where we can stash these people, and let Black Falcon into the building through a window?" Steve asked.

The court clerk nodded. "Judge Tasker's office." She pulled out her lanyard and slipped a key from the plastic casing. "They didn't bother taking this." She grinned and pointed at a nearby door.

"What's your name?"

Aisha could feel his grin behind the helmet. Damn, her brother-in-law could be smooth with the public. Too bad he didn't want to play superhero on a permanent basis.

"Simone," the court clerk said. Her skin was light enough her blush was slightly visible. Yep, he had a way with all the ladies except the one he was truly in love with.

Steve tossed the two minions he'd disabled over his shoulders. "Lead the way, Simone."

"Wait, Ghost Owl." Carol inclined her head toward the two minions Aisha had taken out. "We can't leave them here."

"She's right," Steve said to Aisha in K'iché, the Central American indigenous dialect they both knew between his training for the Peace Corps and her trips to Guatemalan digs with Dad. "They've already seen you move at superspeed."

"I know—" she answered in K'iché before she squeezed her eyes shut for moment. Opening her eyes, she growled under her breath before she hoisted both minions on the floor onto her hips. The other three women stared at her.

"Simone?" Steve prompted.

The court clerk shook herself out of her shock at Aisha's display of superstrength, rushed to the unmarked door, and unlocked it. They followed Simone through the nonpublic hallways to the judge's office she mentioned.

"Black Falcon, we're in the northwest corner office on the third floor," Steve said.

Aisha dumped the two people she carried on the floor. "Ladies, grab phone cords, power cables, anything you can find in this office or the next. We need to tie up these idiots before they wake up."

"Uh, Aisha, would you mind if I simply sit down?" Carol said. "Unless you want to break my shackles, then I could help."

"Sit down." Aisha glared at her client. "I told both you and Harri we're doing this by the book, and I meant it." Carol sat promptly on a visitor chair while Steve lowered the two minions he carried to the utilitarian carpet.

Far more gently than Aisha would have. But then, she struggled with the urge to throw the minions through the dang window.

Simone nudged the court reporter. "Come on, Holly. Let's grab the cords in Celeste's office." The two women departed on their task.

A black shadow appeared in the window. A swell of relief filled Aisha at the sight of Rey in full costume, hovering just outside.

Steve laughed as he pulled something tiny from one of his costume's utility pockets. He held it out to Aisha. She reached out, and he dropped it in her waiting palm.

A comm.

She stuck the device in her ear.

"—throwing a major hissy fit." Nix's voice poured into Aisha's ear. "She's not happy about Black Falcon being up there, and she's even less happy the snipers can't do a damn thing about it."

"Who's not happy?" she asked.

"Consuelo, the new head of Canyon Pointe's FBI office," Arthur said. "Tim's trying to calm her down."

While they talked, Steve used another one of Tim's gadgets to cut a circle, large enough for two humans to fit through, in the window pane. When he finished, Rey tapped the glass. Steve caught the huge piece and set it aside against the judge's bookshelves. Rey flew inside.

As much as she wanted to jump in her husband's arms, she couldn't. This was both their jobs. "Good to see you, Black Falcon."

He nodded. "Ms. Franklin."

She started yanking the cables from the equipment on the judge's desk. Simone and Holly returned with armfuls of cords. The court clerk even had a roll of duct tape.

"If we don't go back into the courtroom with the Ghost Owl and his two guards, their leader is going to know something's wrong," Carol pointed out.

Rey and Steve exchanged looks.

"Crap," Aisha muttered. "She's right." She looked at Rey. "Fly Carol, Holly and Simone down to the authorities."

"No," Carol said sharply. "I'm the only one besides you who's tall enough to fit into their uniforms. Owl and Falcon are way too big to wear the bad guys' clothes"

"No." Aisha slashed the blade of her right hand in the air. "I'm not risking a client's life, especially when she's not a super."

"The jerk who's leading these idiots didn't have one second's hesitation when he shot Marshal Law," Carol snapped back.

Aisha turned back to Rey. "Take the civilians—"

On the floor, two of the minions had been stripped to their skivvies. All four were hog-tied, and their weapons were piled on the desk. Simone and Holly had proud looks on their faces.

"What on earth . . ." Aisha couldn't think of what words to finish with.

"Holly and I were rivals in the rodeo's cattle-roping division when we were in high school." Simone grinned.

"Just never thought I be using those skills on people." Holly quietly high-fived her friend.

"You've helped a great deal, ladies," Rey said. "Now, let's get you two to safety."

He gathered Holly in his arms while Steve picked up a giggling Simone. Carefully, the two men eased the civilians through the hole in the glass before they dived for the street.

"HRSP?" Carol murmured. "And it didn't go away after Mitch was born, did it?"

"I can't talk about it," Aisha muttered. She knelt in front of Carol and broke off her ankle cuffs.

"I've already figured out either Ghost Owl or Black Falcon is Rey, which means the other one is Steve."

Instead of answering, Aisha snapped the cuffs on each of Carol's wrists. The accused attorney stood up and rubbed the marks on her skin.

"Was the original Ghost Owl their father?"

Aisha ignored her and started removing her own clothes. The other attorney should know better than to ask these types of questions.

Carol sighed. "Part of me thought no one could possibly understand why I wanted to protect Pablo and Paul."

Aisha paused and glared at Carol. "Let one of my other clients take you down to the police on the street, or change into minion duds. Either way, shut the fuck up because I haven't kidnapped anyone or plotted their murder."

Carol jerked back, a startled look on her features. Her expression melted into resting bitch face. "Thank you for your honesty, counselor. I guess if I get myself killed, you're off the hook."

Aisha closed her eyes and clenched her fists. Anger and snarky comments were Harri's way of dealing with fear, not hers. When the blood roaring in her ears quieted to a steady stream, she opened her eyes.

"I'm sorry, Carol. My words were uncalled for. I'm scared, and I shouldn't be taking my frustration out on you."

After a moment, the other attorney nodded. "I'm sorry, too. Superpowers aren't the godsend everyone thinks they are."

They both changed clothes quietly. Through the comm, Aisha could hear Rey relaying their plan to Tim.

By the time Aisha and Carol donned the minions' facemasks, the guys slipped back through the hole in the window.

"You don't happen to have an extra comm for Carol, do you?" Aisha asked.

Rey shook his head. "No. Ms. Inunza, if shooting starts, keep Ms. Franklin between yourself and the guns.

Steve held out a key. "Courtesy of Simone. Get the civilians down here through Judge Castillo's entrance in the courtroom. The fire department is bringing around a ladder truck."

"I'm filing a complaint about Consuelo with the FBI regional office when this is over," Aisha grumbled. "We should have more supers on site with the number of hostages."

"You can file all the complaints and personal injury lawsuits you want," Rey said. "Tomorrow after this is over."

The four of them walked back to the unmarked employee entrance to the back offices.

"We're in position, Nix," Rey said. "Give Ghost Owl and our decoy minions twenty seconds."

Aisha's heart pounded as she and Carol escorted Steve down the hallway. As much as she didn't want to go back into that courtroom, there wasn't any choice. Too many lives were at stake. She just prayed Alphahole wouldn't see through hers and Carol's disguise before the rest of the supers played their parts.

CHAPTER 18

Harri hit the floor the instant the doorknob on her office door started to turn. Floor-diving was taking a toll on her dry cleaning bill, but it was better than a bullet wound. Blood was a pain to get out of natural fabrics.

Judge Inunza pulled the trigger. His wild, panicked shot pinged off Cobblestone's broad chest and ricocheted from the steel abstract sculpture on the side table behind Harri before the bullet embedded itself in the drywall less than an inch above her large-screen TV.

Cobblestone rushed the judge, grabbed the handgun, and squeezed the plastic until it shattered. Bright red pieces bounced on the office carpet as they landed. "You okay, Harri?" the super rumbled.

"Yeah." She climbed to her feet and brushed away the couple of pieces of lint that clung to her slacks. "What the ever living hell, Pablo!"

The big, tough criminal judge collapsed to the floor. "It's over. They'll kill my wife and son now."

"Thanks for the save, Cobblestone." Harri smiled at the superhero.

"Ms. Kennedy needed to talk to you." He lumbered back toward the open office door where he dropped his cell phone when Inunza shot at him. Luckily, the device landed on the carpet. He raised it to his left ear. "You still there, Ms. Kennedy?" He held out the phone to Harri.

She accepted it and held it to her own ear. "Susan?"

"Please tell me I didn't hear a gunshot."

Harri grimaced though her partner couldn't see her. "Yeah, you did, but Cobblestone has everything under control."

"I'm heading back to Canyon Pointe," Susan said. "See if you can get Inunza to talk, but I'll bring Mother Defiant with me just in case he doesn't."

"Wait!" Harri blurted. "What are you talking about?"

"I have a strong suspicion our mysterious third party is mine and Aisha's former employers, and they blackmailed the judge to come after you. It wouldn't be the first time they've done something like that. I'll fill you in when we get to the office." The line went dead.

Harri stared at the man on the floor as she handed the phone back to Cobblestone. Inunza wasn't a murderer anymore than his wife. What the hell was Dewey and Cheatham really holding over the judge's head that would make him decide pulling the trigger was a better option than calling the police?

"Pablo, sit on the couch." Harri pointed to the furniture in question. "You and I are still going to have that talk."

"I can't leave you alone in here with him," Cobblestone protested.

"He's not my client, so you can stay," Harri murmured.

"You don't understand." Inunza looked up at her with such sorrow on his face Harri felt sorry for the man. "I've killed them both."

She and her partners may be screwed if she couldn't get the judge to talk. And it looked like it would take some tough love.

"No, you haven't," Harri snapped. "Now, sit on the damn couch before I have Cobblestone make you!"

Inunza blinked like he was surprised someone would raise their voice to him. Cobblestone, on the other hand, snickered. The judge got up off the floor and did as he was told. Harri picked up his coffee, which he'd sat on her desk before pulling out the plastic gun, and handed it to him before resuming her original seat on the couch.

"Now, let's start over again," she said. "Why didn't you and Paul go to the arraignment hearing?"

"Carol asked us not to." The judge sipped his coffee and seemed to be gathering his thoughts. "Paul was upset, but I told him we needed to respect her wishes in the matter."

"Were you at the safe house Special Agent Lewis arranged?" Maybe she'd depended on her ex too much. Maybe his current wife Sarah had a point.

"No." Inunza held up his left palm when Harri opened her mouth. "Don't blame Eddie. His new boss said she couldn't justify the expense, and I agreed with her."

"So you and Paul have been at your house the last three nights?"

The judge nodded.

"No security at all?" Harri asked.

"Only the system I had installed when we moved into our house." A wan smile crossed his face. "Almost nineteen years ago. Carol was six months pregnant with Paul when we bought that house."

"Did you see Paul this morning?"

He nodded. "We ate breakfast together. That's when he said he was working today."

"Did you have any reason to think he was lying?"

Inunza shook his head. "I said maybe he should call off, but he snapped at me. Said if he was going to call off work, it would be to support his mother, not because I was paranoid. He grabbed his keys and left. That was around eight this morning."

"When did you realize something was wrong?"

"When his supervisor from the pool called at eight-forty-five and asked if he could come in." The judge clasped his hands and played with his wedding ring. "At first, I thought he'd gone down to the federal courthouse after all. But I checked the GPS on both his phone and his car. Both were sitting two streets off San Jacinto Avenue. But before I could go check, that's when I got the call from the kidnappers on the house phone. The caller ID was the DA's office."

Tim and Arthur had showed her how easy it was to fake a caller ID. The call could have come from anywhere.

"What did they say?" Harri asked. She took a sip of her coffee. Inunza's whole story sounded like some movie plot. Just too weird to be real. She'd be glad when she could question him with Mother Defiant around.

"The usual BS. Don't call the authorities. Do exactly as we say. If I didn't believe they had both Carol and Paul, I could turn on the news. They also said a service would deliver a package exactly at ten. I was to kill you with the weapon inside."

"So you turned on the news while you waited for the package?" she said.

He nodded. "When I saw the hostage situation at the federal courthouse on Action 12!'s special report, I took the threat seriously."

"Was there anything suspicious about the delivery person who came to your door?"

Again, the judge shook his head. "In fact, the package was two-day ground delivery from here in Canyon Pointe. Whoever these people are, they planned this caper well ahead of time."

"Do you still have the box?" she asked.

"Yes, it's still sitting on our dining room table."

"And what was in the box?" she prompted.

"The plastic gun." He gestured at the remnants of the crushed weapon on her office carpets. "And a bunch of Styrofoam peanuts."

"You need me to get the vacuum and sweep up that mess, Harri?" Cobblestone asked.

"Not yet, but thanks." She turned back to the judge. "What are you supposed to do to prove I killed you?"

"The voice on the phone said he'd know whether or not I did it." He shook his head. "He also said I had until five this evening."

Harri pressed her palms together and rested her index fingers against her lips as she thought. Did these kidnappers know Nella had called here? Tim and Arthur had their phones pretty much tap-proof, but they couldn't protect the TV station's lines. "So they wanted to make the early newscast with all of our deaths."

"What?" the judge said.

"Susan called here because she thinks everything's connected." Harri waved her hand. "The hostage situation, the attempt on her life, and now Paul's kidnapping."

"So what do I do?" Inunza said.

Harri held up her right index finger and set down her coffee. "Let me check something." She rose, crossed to her desk, and opened her comm's case. Slipping the device in her ear, she listened a bit. The good part was the twins had contacted Aisha, The bad part was they were about to launch their rescue plan. She popped the device out and replaced the comm in its case.

"Still busy down at the courthouse?" Cobblestone asked.

"Yeah," she said. "It's going to be just the three of us."

"Rue Liberty is upstairs," Inunza said.

Harri shook her head. "No, she's staying here. Patty needs help protecting the children." She picked up the receiver and dialed Patty's smart phone.

This time, their assistant wasn't chirpy. "Is everything okay downstairs?"

"It is now." Harri glanced at Inunza, but he seemed back to his old self. "Cobblestone and I are stepping out for a bit with Judge Inunza. You got things under control up there?"

"Yeah, we're preparing lunch now."

Harri's stomach chose that moment to growl. "That's not a bad idea."

Patty laughed. "You want PB&J sandwiches and apple slices to take with you?"

Harri couldn't help chuckling, too. "I'll pass for now."

There were voices in the background. "Rue wants to talk to you."

"Harri, take my car," the elderly superhero said. "Cobblestone won't fit in your Honda." Unfortunately, she had a point.

"Thanks, Rue, I appreciate that," Harri murmured. What would this law office and all her people do if Rue Liberty didn't freely offer her assistance? They owed her. They all owed Rue big time.

Patty got back on the line. "Javier's bringing the keys down. And yes, I'll lock everything down again when he's back up here."

"Thanks, Patty. You're the best." Harri hung up and turned to the two men. "We're going on a little field trip, gentlemen. Name your drive-thru."

She crossed her fingers her planned ploy would work, and Howard Dewey didn't call her bluff.

CHAPTER 19

Susan pressed the end call button on her phone. Something had obviously happened with Judge Inunza. Thank goodness Cobblestone was in the building. She really didn't want to be running the law firm by herself if Harri and Aisha got themselves killed.

She looked at Eugenia and Jared. "Pack your bags, people. We're going on a road trip."

Fifteen minutes and one fast food stop later, Susan, Eugenia, and Jared were in her second rental car and headed for the interstate. This was one of those times she was totally jealous of Aisha's power of flight. That girl could travel from Canyon Pointe to Hermanville in an hour. It was going to take Susan roughly two and a half hours by car, but she wanted the supers with her fairly fresh when they arrived.

"I know this is a stupid question," Eugenia said around a mouthful of fries. "But why didn't we just take a commercial flight down?"

"Because our names would show up on the flight manifest." Jared slurped on his shake.

"And someone within the government was behind Captain Justice's betrayal to Professor Paranoia," Susan added. "Which means they probably have some kind of software to flag anyone who isn't on their side."

"It just sounds so far-fetched." Eugenia waved a fry for emphasis. "Like the stupid stories they put out in the comic books about us."

"The SUV that rammed Susan's car this morning wasn't far-fetched," Jared pointed out.

Susan hit the right turn signal in order to merge onto the on-ramp. She checked her rearview mirror, and her heart thudded in her chest. There was a black SUV two cars behind them.

You're just paranoid after this morning's incident, she told herself.

But as she matched speed and melded with the faster traffic, the SUV stayed at a comparable pace. She checked the speedometer. They were traveling at the speed limit. Once they were outside the Hermanville metro area, she could press the gas pedal and see what happened. The state troopers didn't care so much about tickets in the desert between the state's two largest cities.

Jared leaned between the front seats. "You think that's the same guy who tried to kill you this morning?"

"Who?" Eugenia said.

"There's a black SUV that picked us up when we crossed Dillon Street," he said.

Eugenia leaned her head to check the side mirror. "Well, bugger all."

"Bugger all?" Susan bit her lip to keep from laughing.

However, Jared did chuckle. "She's obsessed with *Riverton*, that new British period piece."

"Patty mentioned it." Susan sank deeper into her seat. Talking about mundane things kept her heart from forcing its way up her throat. "I hear the star is pretty hot." She glanced at Eugenia. Pink flushed the super's cheek, and she stared straight ahead.

"Let's just say, I have no complaints." Jared grinned in the rear-view mirror.

"Jared!" Eugenia wailed. Her cheek went from pink to red.

"We live together, babe. It's not like Susan can't figure things out." Jared leaned a little farther between the seats and kissed Eugenia on the cheek.

"I can figure out I'll get ticketed if you don't put your dang seatbelt back on," Susan said.

"Yes, ma'am." He slid back, and a seatbelt clicked.

Traffic started to thin out after a few more miles until it was mainly semis and vacationers headed down to Lake Del Oro for the upcoming holiday weekend. Even though the two cars between her rental and the SUV exited, the big black vehicle stayed the same distance behind her.

"Hang on, you two. I want to test something." Susan pressed the accelerator. When the speedometer reached five miles over the highway's posted limit, she set the cruise control. They gained on the fully loaded eighteen-wheeler in front of her.

She flipped her turn signal and moved into the center lane to go around the truck. Just as she feared, the SUV accelerated. Not enough to be alarming, but enough to keep an eye on her rental. Once the pass was completed, she signaled to move back in the right lane.

"Susan, keep your eyes on the road," Jared said. "I'll watch our shadow."

"Yes, sir." Except there wasn't much mockery in her tone. Jared could outrun the SUV by himself. Inside the car, he was a sitting duck.

"The exit for Silver Gulch is five miles ahead," Eugenia murmured. "Take it."

"There's not much there beside a couple a gas stations, fast food joints, and three cheap motels." Susan glanced at the superhero. There was a grim set to her mouth.

"What's the plan, babe?" Jared asked.

"If they continue past the exit, we'll just get back on the interstate." Eugenia bent forward, pulled a slim silver object from her purse, and handed it back to her boyfriend. "If they don't, you'll stab all four tires on their vehicle while I distract them."

"What about me?" Susan asked.

"You're going to keep our getaway car running," Eugenia said.

"Thank you for not telling me to leave you two alone." Jared patted his girlfriend's shoulder.

"I'm not that stupid," Eugenia growled.

A highway sign whipped by, saying their exit was two miles ahead. Susan's fingers trembled, and she tightened her grip on the steering wheel. If this didn't work, all three of them could die.

That solved the problem of taking over the law firm if Harri or Aisha got themselves killed today.

One mile passed. Up ahead, the overpass for the exit glimmered under the hot summer sun. Susan signaled for the exit and guided her rental into the appropriate lane.

"At the road, turn right and go behind the Uno Inn," Eugenia ordered.

Whatever fear the woman had shown over the lawsuit was gone. This was a superhero in her element.

"It looks empty," Susan said.

"It is," Eugenia answered. "The chain filed for bankruptcy last month. This was one of their closures."

"But no one will be able to see us, either from the road or the interstate," Susan protested.

"Exactly." A vicious smile curved across Mother Defiant's face as she put on her mask.

Both of Susan's passengers had worn their superhero outfits under their street clothes. She didn't know how they tolerated the heat with two layers on. Even with the A/C turned up full blast in her rental car, sweat dampened her back and armpits.

Susan guided her rental into the Uno Inn's parking lot. A quick glance in her rearview mirror showed the SUV turning right from the exit ramp.

So much for wishful thinking.

She drove around the abandoned hotel to the back lot and stopped. Blue Racer was out of the back seat before she put the car into park.

"Stay in the car and keep that engine running no matter what," Mother Defiant ordered. Her veil flapped in the breeze when she exited her seat and stood beside the sedan, waiting for their followers.

Sure enough, the black SUV rounded the building and screeched to a halt when the driver caught sight of Mother Defiant.

Guns pointed out of the front two side windows of the SUV.

Susan squeezed her eyes shut, expecting a shower of bullets to rip through her rental car.

And her body.

Something flashed outside, bright enough it penetrated her eyelids. Men shouted behind the car. The right side doors to her rental opened, and hot air blasted through the interior. She snuck a peak.

Mother Defiant sat beside her and grinned. "Let's go."

Susan glanced in the rearview mirror. Four men stumbled around the SUV with their arms outstretched. All four tires on the other vehicle were flat. Jared had pushed back his Blue Racer cowl and snickered.

"Are they going to be okay?" Susan shifted the gear into drive and accelerated around the building to the road.

"We're heroes." Mother Defiant sniffed. "We don't cause harm."

Susan snorted and took the turn for the interstate onramp at a questionably safe speed. "Don't say that in front of Harri. She'll throw all her cases from when she worked in the Canyon Pointe City Attorneys Office at you to prove you wrong."

"Don't worry." Jared laughed. "A little temporary blindness isn't going to hurt them."

Despite the supers' efforts, Susan kept checking her rearview mirror. She finally began to relax after the fifth mile without a black SUV appearing behind them.

Eugenia must have felt the same because she stripped off her veil, mask, and wimple. Everyone settled back for the long drive to Canyon Pointe. Susan edged the cruise control to ten miles over the speed limit to make up for their little detour at Silver Gulch. Fifteen minutes later, snoring came from the back seat.

The sedan emerged from the shadow of another overpass when something large and colorful landed on the hood. The impact launched the rental into the air.

Susan's last thought as the ground rushed up to meet them was she'd never be able to rent another vehicle from that particular agency ever again.

CHAPTER 20

Aisha gritted her teeth. It felt like spiders were crawling beneath her skin. Rey and Steve had gotten two of the hostages to safety, but there were forty-three other innocent people to worry about.

Forty-four if she counted Carol.

Damn, why had she agreed to let her client stay? Because she might be able to twist it to show the judge Carol wasn't a danger to others if she were granted bail. Still, it was a stupid idea.

The two women escorted Steve down the hallway. A lone minion stood at the main doors to Judge Castillo's courtroom. The minion cocked his head.

"Took you two long enough," the minion said. "Why didn't you signal Azul to shut down the elevator?"

"Really?" When she sneered, Aisha did her best to lower her voice a whole octave. "Split my attention? With him?" She inclined her head toward Steve.

Carol opened the door and pretended to push Steve inside, who added to the illusion by pretending to stumble.

Gasps and murmurs came from the hostages.

"Shut up!" Alphahole shot into the air. Thankfully, the bullet buried itself in the ceiling's plaster. Many of the hostages cried out in fear, but they all huddled on the industrial carpet.

"I'm here," Steve stated. "Let these people go."

"What?" Alphahole laughed. "I'm not letting go of my bargaining chips. Rojo, where's Verde and Morado?"

Aisha shrugged. "How should I know?"

Alphahole and all the other minions froze in place. "Why are you answering Amarillo?"

Oops! Suddenly, all the bad guys' weapons were aimed at her.

Steve's voice whispered through her comm. "Go, go, go."

An earsplitting scream from the other side of the building cut through Aisha's brain, followed by the shattering of glass. Gunshots rang out, which meant Sourpuss and Nix were doing their job of distracting the other minions.

Steve was already moving. His helmet had protected his hearing.

Aisha pushed Carol to the floor and charged the minions to her right. She kicked the first minion she reached into the wall. He crashed through the plasterboard and into the steel support beam with a resounding *BONG*. The contractor would need at least two sheets of new plasterboard, tape, spackle, and paint. The minion may be in the hospital for two-to-three days.

She threw the second minion at the one guarding the door. There was a *crunch* of a bone breaking when they hit before they both crashed into the barrier and rail overlooking the building's atrium. The aluminum bowed and the reinforced glass cracked but held. *Chings* like a cash register rang in her brain.

After she bent the barrel of the third minion's assault rifle, he drew two knives. He threw the first one at her head. She caught it and slammed the bladed into her left palm, crushing it. Well, that was two pieces of expensive hardware destroyed.

Oh, god, she was turning into Harri, counting damage from supers.

Aisha punched the minion in the face and broke their jaw. The *chings* continued. Considered these jerks had shot at least two federal employees, she'd feel bad about the damage she was inflicting later.

Another shot rang out, and everyone paused. All the minions were down. The hostages were gone. All except Carol and Judge Castillo. And Carol's mask was on the floor.

Alphahole had one arm wrapped around Carol's neck and held his handgun to her temple. "Stand down, or I'll blow out her brains."

"I said take me," Judge Castillo growled. "She's just a perp. The FBI will open fire the second you try to leave with her. I'm a more valuable hostage."

"Carol Inunza is way more valuable to me," Alphahole sneered. "It wouldn't look good if Franklin lost her to a supervillain."

"You are not a supervillain," Steve said.

"You're not helping," Aisha hissed.

"He's not a supervillain any more than he was when he pretended to be a homeless man in Founder's Green," Steve continued in a mocking tone. "He is and he will always be Trubble's little kiss-ass. He's jealous Black Death replaced him as the general's favorite pet assassin. The only question is who's holding Dante Valentine's leash now."

"Valentine?" Aisha cocked her head. "You mean Crazy Jim? The asshat who tried to strangle Harri?"

"Yeah," Steve said. "And he couldn't even do that right. Why Trubble didn't shoot him between the eyes is beyond me."

"Why the hell are you after the original Ghost Owl?" Aisha asked.

"Because Trubble's obsessed," Carol said. "And Valentine wants back in Trubble's good graces."

"What on earth are you all blabbing about?" Judge Castillo threw his arms in the air.

"Byron S. Trubble, the former head of the black ops organization Corvus, blames the original Ghost Owl for his downfall," Aisha said. "He also stupidly believes the original Owl is the supposedly dead grandson of Eagle Forever."

"What does Eagle Forever have to do with any of this?" The judge appeared totally flabbergasted.

"It's daddy issues." Steve managed to exhibit his total disgust even with the vocalizer in his helmet. "Eagle Forever was Trubble's mentor, but they disagreed over the government taking control of children with superpowers. My predecessor had reason to believe Trubble kidnapped many of the children destined for the government training facility."

"Black Death was one of those children," Aisha added. "Unfortunately, he's so indoctrinated by Trubble he can't see he's being used. But Valentine here didn't have the loyalty to go down with his boss like Black Death did."

"And I have to thank Winters and Franklin for getting Trubble out of my way." Valentine backed toward the judge's entrance into the court room, dragging Carol along with him. "I'll be much richer for it."

A dark shadow appeared on the open door to the back hallway. Part of a crimson and black helmet peered around the corner.

The comm in Aisha's ear crackled to life. "All the hostages arrre out but three," Sourpuss said. "We're starrrting the clean-up."

"Stay back," Rey murmured. Thankfully, he could silence his external speaker to answer Sourpuss. "We've got a gun on a female hostage in the courtroom."

"Rrrogerrr," Sourpuss replied.

"We didn't exactly do it for you, but you could have bought yourself a place on Mal Paraíso Island." Aisha replied to Valentine's statement.

"Who'd want to live with those losers?" Valentine said.

Aisha laughed. "So you and Trubble pissed off a bunch of supervillains, too? Or were they more children you two tortured until they broke and became worthless to you?" She waved her hand at his minions. "Either way, it doesn't matter. All of your people are incapacitated, Valentine. It's over."

"You wanna play 'Let's Make a Deal', Franklin?" Valentine paused in his retreat. "How about you let me go, and I won't tell everyone you got knocked up by Captain Justice? And by the way, Captain Justice is still alive."

Both Carol and Judge Castillo stared at Aisha. Her fears about the revelation of her husband and son's secrets were coming to life. For the first time, she really understood what drove Carol to commit the crimes she had.

The other attorney collected herself and rolled her eyes. "*Ese*, everyone knows that! You want some real dirt about her, take me with you." Then she winked.

"Carol!" Aisha yanked off the knit mask and played along. "I represented you pro bono! How could you do this to me?"

"I can tell you who the new Ghost Owl is," Carol said.

"I really don't give a rat's ass about him," Valentine growled.

"I can also tell you who the original Ghost Owl, too," Carol added.

Aisha could see greed fill Valentine's eyes. "Tell me."

"Not until you and I make a deal," Carol said.

"I'll let you walk away alive." He pressed his gun into her temple hard enough she cried out.

"Don't hurt her." Judge Castillo held up his hands. Blood from his bailiff smeared the sleeves and chest of his white dress shirt. "She and Franklin are trying to protect me."

Valentine slowly twisted until he and Carol faced Judge Castillo. "What are you talking about?"

"I'm the one you want." Castillo's whole body seemed to droop. "I'm the original Ghost Owl."

CHAPTER 21

Burritos from Marta's restaurant satisfied the rumbling in both Harri and Cobblestone's stomachs. Judge Inunza claimed he wasn't hungry, but that didn't stop him from munching on the chicken taquitos Harri ordered for him. Their next stop was the street where the GPS said Paul's car still sat.

"Rue Liberty's ride ain't half-bad," Cobblestone said from the backseat. "I may need to get me one of these babies."

"You do know this car is older than the judge here." Harri grinned. "You might have a hard time finding one that's in good shape."

"Do you really want to go there, Ms. Winters?" the judge warned.

She glanced at him before returning her attention to the traffic around them. He was sounding more like himself, but there was still a thick layer of worry in his voice.

"Let's face it, Your Honor." She slowed for the upcoming red light. "The cars built when we were kids weren't the best engineered vehicles on the road. But finding decent cars older than that are becoming next to impossible."

Her comment lightened his mood, and he chuckled. "Touché, Counselor."

The light turned green. She accelerated and wove through the heavy midday traffic until she turned onto San Jacinto Avenue. This was the original Main Street when her ancestors first laid out the plots and thoroughfares of what eventually became Canyon Pointe.

San Jacinto retained its independent character of the first settlers. Cute little specialty stores lined the streets with the occasional bodega every two or three blocks. The oldest church in the state, a national historic landmark, still held services. Harri turned onto Little Elm Lane.

"There's Paul's car." The judge pointed ahead of them. "The little blue car."

Like she could have missed the electric blue pocket rocket.

She pulled into the empty parking spot behind the car. Inunza had the door open and was out of the ancient sedan before either Harri or Cobblestone could stop him. The judge pulled out keys from his left pocket. The pocket rocket's lights blinked and horn honked when he unlocked it.

"Serves him right if he blows himself up," Cobblestone grumbled. Inunza opened the door of his son's car and slid into the driver's seat.

Harri looked over her shoulder at the superhero. He played down his intelligence so much she sometimes forgot how smart he really was. "You think the kidnappers sabotaged Paul's car?"

"Probably not," Cobblestone admitted. "If he came here first, he couldn't kill you."

Harri chuckled as she and Cobblestone climbed out of Rue's car. They crossed over to the pocket rocket and looked inside while Inunza unlocked the glove box. Inside were a ton of ketchup packets, a wad of napkins, and a smart phone.

The judge pulled out the phone and stared at it a moment before he looked up at Harri. "This doesn't make sense. Why would the kidnappers take the time to lock up Paul's phone?"

"The kid may not have been snatched here." Cobblestone rubbed his chin. "Or, and I hate to say this, sir, but your son may be up to something."

Harri looked at the superhero over the top of the car. "That's not Paul. He makes R—" She stopped herself just in time. Cobblestone may know Rey's secret identity, but Judge Inunza didn't. "Black Falcon look like Al Capone."

The judge climbed out of his son's car. "Let's check the house. If this is all a stupid teenage prank because he's angry with me, that boy's going to be grounded until he's ninety."

⌇

Silence reigned in Rue Liberty's antique sedan the rest of the way to the judge's house. The two-story home was located in one of the older neighborhoods of Canyon Pointe along the Rio Diaz. The builders kept many of the old growth cottonwood trees, which shaded the large yards and kept the grass alive in the city's arid climate.

Harri pulled into the judge's driveway and put the gear in park. Before she could turn off the ignition, Cobblestone reached over the back of the front bench seat and laid a huge hand on her arm.

"You two, stay here. Keep the engine running while I check out the property." He opened the passenger door. "If I'm not back in ten minutes, go straight to the Lechuza Building. Judge, what's your security code?"

"Five, nine, one, three," Inunza answered.

The shocks bounced the car when Cobblestone got out of it. He gently closed the door and lumbered around the attached garage.

Harri sighed at being benched, but the superhero was right. Whoever tried to blackmail Inunza might be inside, waiting for his return. On the plus side, Rue Liberty kept her car's A/C in perfect condition.

The judge leaned his forearms on the dash and stared at his home. "Is this what your typical day is like, Harri?"

She burst out laughing. "Only over the last year."

"You miss working for the city?" There seemed to be some kind of implication in his words.

She shifted in her seat to look at him. "What are you getting at, Pablo?"

"You could get your old job back with a hefty salary increase." He grinned. "Mayor Benevides is realizing how much money you retrieved for Canyon Pointe for damages from all the supers."

"Uh-huh," she drawled. "What you mean is the idiot they hired to replace me can't find his dick with both hands and a searchlight. He hasn't been able to touch any of my clients. He managed to foul up the case against Steelrose last fall and forced the D.A. to let her go scot-free. And we both know the city council won't authorize a junior attorney to assist me. Yeah, I really want to beg for my old job back."

Inunza shrugged. "Al just asked me to feel you out the next time I saw you."

Understanding of his real objective whispered through Harri. He was trying to focus on anything to keep his mind off his family.

"Paul's a smart kid. If he gets a chance to run for help, he will. And that's assuming he's really in trouble."

"If only it were that easy," Inunza murmured.

The front door of the house opened. Cobblestone stepped out on the porch and beckoned for them to come inside.

"Let's go." Harri flipped off the ignition, yanked on the handle, and shoved open the heavy driver-side door. There was probably more metal in the door than there was in her entire car.

She locked up the car once the judge had exited it. Together, they strode across the sidewalk and up the porch steps.

"Doesn't look like anyone's been in here since the judge left," Cobblestone said. "But I ain't a detective."

"Where's the box?" Harri asked.

"In here." Inunza led the way through the formal living room into a formal dining room. He hadn't been joking about the amount of Styrofoam peanuts either. They were scattered across the polished maple hardwood surface of the table. The standard medium-sized brown cardboard shipping box lay on its side.

"Should we check it for fingerprints?" Cobblestone asked.

"I doubt it would do any good," Harri mused. "The whole point of sending it through a commercial service was to obliterate and confuse any prints or DNA on the box."

She set the box upright and folded the flaps together to see the label. Instead of a typical printed address, there was a QR code in the sender spot. She pulled out her phone and scanned the code, praying that it didn't trigger something disastrous on her cell.

Harri breathed a sigh of relief when the name of a local independent shipping and office supply shop popped up on her screen. "It was sent from Ship 'n' Such on MLK and Twelfth Street."

"But they would have hundreds of packages going out every day," Cobblestone protested.

"You may have the flashy, video-worthy career, my friend." Harri grinned. "But my specialty is good, old-fashioned investigative work, which most times is boring as hell."

"To Ship 'n' Such?" Inunza raised a questioning right eyebrow.

Harri gathered the box under her arm. "To Ship 'n' Such."

When they got to the store twenty minutes later, Harri wondered if this was such a good idea. The place reeked of pot smoke, and from the glazed look of the kid with the straggly beard behind the counter, he'd inhaled all of it.

"My computer says the package was delivered on time," the kid protested.

"I need the *record* of *this* sale," she repeated for the third time as she tapped the barcode for the unique shipping record. "Who brought the box in to be shipped?"

"I gotta get the manager." The kid sauntered back through the beaded curtain to the employee area.

"I don't mind a joint once in a while, but obviously, all the PSAs I did had no effect," Cobblestone grumbled.

"The pot laws were written to put people like us in jail, *ese*," Inunza answered.

Cobblestone chuckled. "And here I thought you were wound so tight you snapped."

All humor disappeared from the judge. "Only when it comes to my family."

The kid returned through the curtain. A slight blond girl followed him.

"Hi!" She flashed a bright smile. "Oh, wow! Cobblestone! I'm a huge fan. Can I get a selfie with you?" Her fellow co-worker blinked and stared dumbly at the superhero.

"After you answer this lady's questions." Cobblestone pointed his thumb at Harri.

"Owen said you had a problem with a package you received?" the girl asked.

"We need to find out who mailed this package." Harri pointed at the bar code. Again.

The girl grabbed a handheld scanner and looked at the screen. A scowl replaced her bright smile. "I can't tell you who he is. He always pays cash."

"What about a description of this man?" the judge asked.

Her expression shifted immediately to suspicion. "You two cops?"

"No, they're friends of mine," Cobblestone said. "The man who paid you cash sent something illegal through the shipping service. We only need the information, and we promise not to mention you and Owen when we do go to the cops."

The girl muttered an obscenity. "He always brings his packages pre-sealed. He's older. Dyes his hair brown but it never matches his toupee. Always wears expensive suits. He's kind of pervy. He always hits on me." She shuddered.

"White?" Harri asked.

The girl nodded.

There was only one male at Dewey and Cheatham who fit that

description, and he wasn't even an attorney. Harri pulled up the rival firm's website on her phone, found the right profile, and held her device up for the girl to see the screen. "Is this him?"

The girl shuddered again. "Yeah," she said with a healthy amount of disgust.

"Thanks . . ." Harri raised an eyebrow.

"Mia."

Harri pulled out a couple of large bills from her wallet and handed them to Mia. "Don't let Owen smoke the money."

"Wow! Thanks!" From her smile, Harri had made her day.

"Still want that picture, Mia?" Cobblestone said.

"Definitely!" She circled around the counter and pulled out her smart phone. Cobblestone took a couple of photos with her.

At Owen's disappointed expression, Cobblestone took pity on the kid. "You want one, too, *ese?*"

"Can I really?" It was the closest to any animation Owen displayed during their visit.

"Sure." Cobblestone grinned.

After another round of cell phone pictures and Cobblestone's permission to post one of the photos of him with both Mia and Owen on the store bulletin board, Harri left with the box and her charges.

She shook her head as they approached Rue Liberty's huge sedan. "I need to have you teach a superheroes clinic on dealing with the public."

Cobblestone chuckled. "I remember being star struck when I was younger than Mia and Owen. Captain Portent was kind to me. I wanted to be just like him."

Harri smiled. And Rey wanted to do charitable work like Cobblestone in addition to superheroing. "There's more than a few supers and civilians who look at you the same way."

"What's next, Counselor?" Inunza asked.

"You'll enjoy this part, Judge." Her grin widened. "We're going to rattle Stuart Cheatham's cage."

CHAPTER 22

This time, the airbags deployed when Susan's second rental hit the pavement and rolled. Glass shattered. Somehow, the car landed with its wheel-side down.

"That was Steelrose." Eugenia gasped.

"Are you hurt?" Susan asked.

"Arm's broken."

Susan looked over at the superhero and nearly threw up on herself. Bloody bone poked out of the skin of Eugenia's forearm.

"Jared?"

Susan carefully twisted to look in the back seat. He was out cold with blood trickling from a large cut on his forehead. She looked around, but she couldn't find her purse.

Which meant her taser was totally useless.

She swallowed hard. They needed to get out of this car, but she couldn't carry Blue Racer by herself.

With a screech of metal, the driver side door disappeared momentarily before it landed thirty feet in front of her rental. Steelrose poked her head inside.

"Hey there, fishy, fishy, fishy." Her teeth gleamed gold in the afternoon light. The supervillain could turn her skin into any type of metal. Too bad Sparx wasn't with them. One of her blasts of lightning could overload Steelrose.

Instead, a red laser light hit the supervillain right between her eyes. She screeched and stumbled back a few steps.

"Run, Susan," Mother Defiant hissed. She had already unbuckled her seat. Aiming her right index finger at the twisted metal the passenger door had become, she emitted another wave of laser light to slice through the wreckage.

Susan hit the release on her own seatbelt and scrambled out of the car. If she could distract the supervillain for a moment, maybe Blue Racer would wake up.

Or maybe she'd find her purse.

Or maybe she'd simply die.

A hard, cold hand grabbed the back of her neck after she'd taken four steps. "Where ya goin', Red?" Steelrose started to squeeze. "You're my meal ticket."

Spots swam in Susan's vision. The pain pierced her brain and she screamed.

Steelrose screamed, too. Susan hit the hard, packed earth. The impact knocked any oxygen out of her lungs.

"You bitch!" the supervillain roared. "You want a taste, Miss Goody Two Shoes?" She charged toward the rental.

Susan tried to stand but only got as far as her hands and knees. Her muscles decided to remind her about the morning accident. Yards away, Steelrose stalked Mother Defiant, whose skin was as white as her wimple, around the remnants of the second rental car. Susan didn't see Blue Racer anywhere. He had to still be in the back seat, unconscious.

Crap. Susan searched for anything she could use as a weapon. Rocks weren't going to do anything to Steelrose's hide. Neither would the plastic fender or the shattered bits of a side mirror.

"Lady, are you okay..." Steelrose and Mother Defiant's presence registered in the brain of Susan's would-be rescuer.

"Call 9-1-1," Susan ordered. Her phone remained in her pocket despite the tumbling car. She pulled it out and thumbed to the self-destruct. After everything that had happened over the last year, Tim and Arthur didn't want any of their software or tech falling into the wrong hands, so they added a timer that would blow the lithium batteries. She wasn't sure how bad it would hurt Steelrose, or even if it would.

But it was the only thing she had.

She looked up at the man who helped to her feet. "Tell them there's an ongoing superhero-supervillain battle southbound just past Exit 153, and get everybody as far from me as possible." She started jogging as best as she could away from her rental. Away from her clients. Away from the civilian motorists who had stopped along the interstate to render aid.

When she couldn't go any further, she turned around slowly because her dizziness was getting worse. "Hey! Stankrose! Why are you messing with her? I'm your contract!"

Steelrose's attention flipped between Susan and Mother Defiant. It finally dawned on the supervillain that Mother Defiant wasn't going anywhere. With a malicious grin on her shiny mug, Steelrose raced toward Susan.

She pressed the button on her phone to start the five second countdown. Steelrose was closing fast.

At three, Susan yelled, "Catch!" and threw the phone as hard as she could. To her surprise, Steelrose actually caught the damn thing, but Susan was already diving for a slight depression in the desert soil. She squeezed her eyes shut as she hit the sand and stones and covered her head with her arms.

The light and intense heat washed over her before the sound rattled her aching bones. The rain of dirt and rocks came next. Finally, silence.

Off in the distance, there was shouting. Someone touched her shoulder.

Susan carefully lifted her head. It was the motorist who first approached her.

"Troopers are on their way." He looked at something to her right. "Told them that the heroes were down, but a civilian took out Steelrose." He shook his head. "Maybe next time, the stupid lawyers and judges won't let her off on a technicality when she robs a bank."

CHAPTER 23

Before Aisha could say anything, Carol cried out, "Frank! Shut up! Now's not the time to—"

"This isn't worth your life, Carol." Judge Castillo addressed Valentine. "I used to date Harri Winters. We were better as friends than as a couple. I'm getting too old to work during the day and run around battling crime at night." He tried to subtly gesture to Steve. "So, she helped me recruit the kid."

Valentine laughed. "Good one, man. You are not a super."

"You're right," Castillo said. "I'm not. I grew up in the slums north of the Canyon Block. The licensed supers have never given a shit about that side of the city. So I did something about the criminals who preyed on the people. Why do you think they call me Jatz'om Kuh? Because I'm the fucking king of the Northside!"

The judge's impassioned speech almost had Aisha believing him.

From the way Valentine twitched, he was buying Castillo's story, too.

"You'd figured out my secret identity," the judge said. "That's the real reason why you hit my court this morning, isn't it? You planned to use my own attorney against me?" He gestured at Aisha.

"Wasn't that obvious?" Valentine sneered. Compared to the judge, the former Corvus assassin's acting sucked.

"What do you think you're going to get out of me, son?" Castillo lowered his hands. "I'm not worth whatever they're paying you. And that's assuming they actually pay you."

Valentine hesitated. The same thoughts must have been running through his excuse for a brain.

Castillo looked at Aisha again. "Let me guess. Seismic Shift's destruction of the Lake County Retirement Home was no accident."

"No, it wasn't," Aisha said quietly. "They targeted your grandfather Forever Eagle. That's the reason Trubble's paranoid. The proverbial roosters are coming home."

Castillo faced Valentine. "Is it worth going down for Trubble? It sure sounds to me like he hung you out to dry."

"No." A ferociousness laced Valentine's voice. Or maybe it was just plain craziness. "You volunteered so I'll take you with me, Judge. I'll get a pretty penny for you. And if you aren't the original Ghost Owl, well, then, I'll take Franklin's suggestion. I hear Mal Paraíso is lovely this time of year."

Valentine shoved Carol away from him in preparation for yanking the judge closer as a body shield. Carol half-fell, half-threw herself onto the floor.

In that split second, Rey entered the room. He grabbed the handgun out of Valentine's hand, breaking a couple of fingers from the firecracker *SNAP*s. Rey squeezed the weapon like putty and placed Valentine in handcuffs before the supervillain wannabe's first howl echoed through the courtroom. And to top it off, the wuss passed out from the pain.

Aisha released a breath of relief. "Sourpuss, situation up here is resolved, and the gunman is cuffed."

"FBI and I arrre on ourrr way up," the superhero said in Aisha's ear.

Castillo leaned over, clasped Carol's hand, and helped her to her feet. "Are you all right?"

She chuckled. "Other than rug burn on my chin and a few bruises from both my attorney and the terrorists throwing me on the floor. Yeah. I'm fine." She turn to Aisha. "So, do you people take turns playing the Ghost Owl?"

Before she could answer, Steve approached the judge. "Your Honor, you shouldn't have played the Ghost Owl card."

"You going to sue me for trademark infringement?" Castillo asked.

"There's some very dangerous people who have tried to abduct and kill me since my mentor died." Steve turned toward Carol. "Isn't that so Ms. Inunza?"

Aisha had to bite the inside of her lip to keep from laughing. Carol's incredulous expression flicked from Steve's gray visor to Aisha and back a couple of times. "The confrontation in my office was one big con job?"

"Don't kidnap my partner again, and I won't borrow my client's outfit to knock you out," Aisha said with mock seriousness. However, her mood quickly shifted to real solemnity. "I'm sorry, but the guys and I have to turn you back over to the feds until your arraignment can be rescheduled."

"I know." Her expression turned bleak. "Technically, we're ex parte right now."

"Black Falcon, Ghost Owl, would you please escort Ms. Inunza and Judge Castillo out to the EMTs and have them checked out?" Aisha said. "I'll coordinate with Nix, Sourpuss, and the authorities."

Her husband and brother-in-law both nodded and guided their charges out of the wrecked courtroom over their protests of leaving Aisha alone with a bunch of unconscious minions. Heck, if one of them awoke, she'd be sorely tempted to knock them out again.

Her comm crackled, and Tim said, "Aisha, you clear?"

She retreated to the doorway to the judge's chambers where she could talk and still keep an eye on the unconscious minions. "Clear. What's going on?"

"There's reports of a super battle on the interstate between here and Hermanville, and we just got the notice Susan activated the self-destruct on her phone from that same location."

Aisha couldn't breathe. She slumped against the doorjamb. How could this day get any worse?

CHAPTER 24

After setting up her phone to record the conversations she was about to have, Harri stalked into the offices of Dewey and Cheatham, LLP, with a superhero and a judge trailing behind her. Yet, she felt as if she had an army.

The place looked the same as it had when Aisha worked here. Well, except the wall paint had been updated to the latest designer color. And like every other time Harri visited, there was a new girl sitting at the receptionist desk.

Mia at Ship 'n' Such wasn't wrong about Stuart Cheatham's perviness. He was the reason the law firm went through so many receptionists and assistants and had so few female associates.

"How can I help you?" the girl at the receptionist desk chirped.

"You can't," Harri said equally cheerfully. She headed down the hallway to Stuart's corner office. If she could break him, he'd turn on Howard Dewey in a heartbeat.

"Excuse me! Ma'am! You can't go back there!"

"Stop me!" Harri yelled over her shoulder.

"I'll call the police!" the receptionist shrieked.

"Please do, Miss," Cobblestone said behind her.

Harri reached Stuart's door and twisted the knob, but it was locked. She looked at Cobblestone.

"You paying my bail and fines," the superhero said.

"Honey, I will pay for your next children's health fair on the north side," she answered.

Cobblestone reared back and kicked Stuart's door with his massive foot. The fiberboard around the lock splintered. The door flew open.

"What the hell!" Stuart Cheatham jumped to his feet. His erection poked out from under his dress shirt. From the skirted ass and stilettos sticking out from under Stuart's desk, Harri could guess why.

Harri stalked into Stuart's office. She motioned for Cobblestone to push the door shut. He complied and stood so he blocked the view through the broken fiberboard.

"Young lady under the desk," Harri said. "Stand up, straighten your clothes, then head to the ladies room to fix your makeup."

The younger woman slowly stood up, but she wouldn't meet Harri's eyes. Her cheeks flushed pink.

"Deedee Lawson?" Inunza blurted.

The younger woman's cheeks flared red as she buttoned her blouse. She still wouldn't meet anyone's gaze.

Harri leaned closer to the judge. "Who is she?"

"She interned in my court two years ago."

Harri ground her teeth. There were so many things she wanted to say, but right now, she needed to focus on Paul. Or was there some way to work this to her favor?

She pulled a business card from her purse. The cards were an old-fashioned touch, but they worked. She marched over to the younger woman.

"If you need to talk, call me," Harri murmured. "In fact, why don't we go out for dinner tonight?"

Deedee finally looked up at Harri. Mascara and tears trailed down the girl's cheeks. It was obvious things with Stuart weren't mutual.

"You can't—" he blurted.

"Shut up, Stuart," Harri ground out. "And pull up your damn pants."

If Miguel wasn't on a contracting job, she call him to pick up Deedee. Harri fished in her purse for a pen and scribbled Marta's name and the address of the restaurant on the back of the card.

"You have a car?" Harri asked.

Deedee swallowed hard and nodded.

"Go here. Tell them I sent you. They'll take good care of you." Harri wanted to hug the younger woman, but she didn't dare. Deedee looked like she could shatter at any moment. "Go now."

Harri glared at Stuart. "And if your pay gets docked, call me."

Cobblestone opened the office door, and Deedee fled like a flock of Professor Triassic's velociraptors chased her. The superhero closed the door.

Harri flopped into one of the leather chairs across the desk from Stuart and glared at him. At least, the idiot had zipped up.

"I heard through the grapevine the Ghost Owl already had a little talk with you about threatening the Dewey and Cheatham staff in return for sexual favors, Stuart."

The so-called development manager trembled. It was a position his father made up for him when he couldn't even pass the bar exam after five tries. If the idiot didn't have a trust fund, he'd be hanging out with the other homeless on Founder's Green.

"I'll pass today's incident on to him unless you answer some questions," she said.

"You can pass on anything you want, but he can't really do anything to me," Stuart sneered. "He's a registered super. The Owl can't touch me."

"You're right. The Owl can't," Cobblestone rumbled. "But it would be a shame if you jumped to your death after getting caught raping an associate."

Stuart's pasty face developed a green tint. He shook in earnest, and a damp splotch on the front of his pants grew.

"What the hell, man?" Inunza said in Spanish.

"I wasn't going to throw him through the window," Cobblestone answered in kind. "I ain't spending the rest of my life in Mauvaises." For once, Harri was glad Aisha insisted she brushed up on her Spanish because Aisha and Rey wanted Mitch raised bilingual.

From the look on Stuart's face, he didn't understand a single word the two men said except for the name of the prison.

"I-I'm not a super." Stuart collapsed in his office chair. "Y-you can't send me there."

Harri chuckled. "First of all, anyone can be sent to Mauvaises if the prosecutor petitions the judge based on your crimes. And you and Howard have blackmailed your last judge."

"I didn't say anything to Judge Inunza," Stuart blurted.

"Who said it was me?" Inunza claimed the chair next to Harri.

"I-uh-I-I—" Stuart looked like he was about to have a stroke.

"We have a witness who saw you enter and leave the Ship 'n' Such store on MLK two days ago," Harri said. "We've got the box you sent. All I have to do is tell the DA, and he'll get a warrant."

"You can't prove it was me." Stuart raised his voice. "I paid with cash."

Yep, confronting Stuart first was the best decision she'd made all day.

"Do you know what the penalty is for mailing any firearm?" the judge said.

"Firearm?" Stuart's eyes bugged out. "I thought it was paperwork and a video."

"Is that what Howard Dewey told you?" Harri asked.

For the first time, Stuart clamped his jaw shut.

Inunza looked at Harri. "We might as well call the FBI. Sending a firearm through the mail will net this bozo a couple of decades."

"It didn't go through the U.S. Mail," Stuart sneered. "The box went through ParcelPlus."

"Then who packed the gun in the box, Stuart?" Harri asked.

Once again, Stuart clamped his jaw shut.

"Son," Inunza said, though there was at most a dozen years' difference between the men's ages. He leaned forward. "You've already given us enough here to spend a couple of decades behind bars. You cooperate, and the three of us will use our collective pull to cut you a deal with the feds."

Stuart fidgeted for a full minute before he sunk lower into his office chair. "What do you want to know?"

"Where's my son, Paul?"

Stuart blinked. "He's in Howard's office signing a major licensing deal."

Out of everything Harri expected in this encounter, the words "Paul" and "licensing deal" hadn't even entered the equation.

CHAPTER 25

"You don't understand." Susan waved her arms at the trooper who was questioning her. "The same person who hired Steelrose to kill me plans to murder my law partners. We have to get to Canyon Point now!"

Trooper Hanscum pulled off her hat and wiped at the perspiration on her forehead. The blond wisps that had escaped her tight bun were soaked with perspiration. She replaced her hat.

"Ms. Kennedy, your firm represents supers, right?" She gestured at the ambulance where Blue Racer and Mother Defiant were being treated. "Can't your partners call in one or two of them to help?"

Susan seethed internally, but she managed to keep her voice level. "Ms. Winters has Cobblestone looking after her, but Ms. Franklin is being held hostage along with a bunch of civilians at the federal courthouse in Canyon Pointe. Last I heard, the new head of the FBI office isn't letting any supers get involved."

"Maybe she has a point." Hanscum gestured at the remnants of the rental scattered across the desert dirt.

"If the people are who we suspect they are, they could be out of the country before the hostage situation is resolved," Susan said.

"Why don't you tell me—" Hanscum started.

"With all due respect, ma'am, the bad guys have a mole in law enforcement," Blue Racer said, turning on the charm. "That's how Captain Justice died last year. It's nothing personal. I'm sure you are a fine, upstanding member of law enforcement. But all it will take is the wrong word in the wrong ear, and a lot of people will die."

Finally, Hanscum nodded. "All right."

Susan waited breathlessly as the state trooper relayed the request to her sergeant. The trooper's radio crackled. The sergeant asked, "Does this have anything to do with the hostage situation at the federal courthouse?"

"Yes, sir," Susan and the trooper said at the same time.

"All right. Chopper's on its way to the scene of the accident. The NSB wagon says they're ten minutes out. Has Steelrose woken up?"

Hanscum glanced at the supervillain who looked like a mummy on the desert sand. Her arms and legs had been wrapped in a special Tyvek tape by the other troopers. It was more secure for supers than traditional steel cuffs.

Especially for those who could easily snap said restraints.

"No, sir. She's still out cold," the trooper reported.

"Copy that," her sergeant said, and the radio went silent.

"Mother Defiant, we really need to take you back to Hermanville," the paramedic treating her said. "That's the closest trauma center."

"No!" she snapped. "I'm going to Canyon Pointe, so set my arm here, or shut up."

Susan winced. All that time she and Aisha spent coaching the superhero had flown out the car window with her purse. "Mother, I know you're in a lot of pain, but you can't take it out on the first responders."

Mother Defiant's bottom lip quivered. "Would you set my arm, please?"

"Look, I'm not trying to upset you." The paramedic held up his gloved hands. "But I'm going to need you to sign the paperwork that says you're acting against medical advice."

Mother Defiant was obviously about to say something impolite, so Susan cleared her throat.

Instead, the superhero smiled and nodded. "I understand. I won't hold anything against you."

Trooper Hanscum eyed Susan. "Ms. Kennedy, I've got a report here that says you were involved in a hit-and-run this morning."

"Yes." Susan grimaced. "It was the first attempt to kill me today."

The state trooper continued asking questions about the earlier incident until Mother Defiant yelled, "Susan isn't the supervillain here!"

"Do you want to spend the night in jail for obstruction of justice?" Hanscum replied.

"Try it, and see what happens," Mother Defiant shot back.

Susan stepped between the two women. "She's in a lot of pain, Trooper. She's not in her right mind."

"She's never in her right mind," Hanscum spat.

"What's that supposed to mean?" Mother Defiant yelled at the same time, Susan asked, "What are you talking about?"

"My daughter decided she needed to go Catholic school because of her." Trooper Hanscum jabbed her index finger at Mother Defiant. "Do you have any idea how much a private school costs? We're not even Catholic!"

"Can we please focus on this incident?" Susan asked.

"It seems to be a pattern." Hanscum looked at her tablet. "You sure do get into a lot of accidents, Ms. Kennedy, but never with your own vehicle."

Irritation crawled along Susan's skin. "What's that supposed to mean?"

Hanscum cocked her head. "I have to wonder if you're not trying to scam some of these rental places with your so-called accidents."

"They're not accidents when supervillains and minions deliberately trash my rental cars!" Susan wanted to throttle the trooper herself.

"I know you're upset, Ms. Kennedy, but you can't take it out on law enforcement." Blue Racer wore an impish grin as the other paramedic stitched up the cut on his forehead.

"Stay out of this," Susan snapped at the superhero. She turned back to Trooper Hanscum, took a deep breath, and released it. "Can you and I sit in your car, and you can finish your questioning? I think the sun's getting to me."

"Sure." The trooper nodded.

Once the women were ensconced in the blessed coolness of Hanscum's patrol car, the trooper looked at Susan.

"I apologize. I shouldn't have said what I did back there."

Susan chuckled weakly. "Mother Defiant has the tendency to get on a lot of people's nerves, including my own partners.'"

"I just wanted to say I'm not anti-Catholic. And my daughter did get an academic scholarship at Saint Eugenia's." Hanscum squeezed her hands into fists, and then stretched out her fingers. "I've run into Mother Defiant before, and she just-she just—"

"Comes across as holier-than-thou?" Susan offered.

"Yeah," the trooper admitted.

"I shouldn't say this, but do you want to know who provided your daughter's scholarship?"

Hanscum's eyes widened. "You're messing with me?"

Susan shook her head. "I don't know all the details, but Mother Defiant had a rough childhood. The sisters at Saint Eugenia's were the closest thing she had to stability. She was eating mac and cheese rather than miss a payment to the school, which was why she hired me to increase her licensing deals." She shrugged. "I'm still working on increasing her manners."

Hanscum whistled. "I guess there's more going on under their costumes than the public realizes."

"There usually is," Susan admitted.

The NSB armored truck arrived just as Hanscum finished with her questions. Susan gritted her teeth as she climbed out of the trooper's patrol car. It figured Agent Wilbur Nesmith would be the one to command the scene. He seemed to have taken a special interest in Winters and Franklin's clients.

"Agent Nesmith," she said as she approached the man.

"Ms. Kennedy." He inclined his head. "Seems like your entire staff of attorneys are in a bit of a jam today."

She waved toward the ambulance. "That's why there's a helicopter on its way to take Mother Defiant, Blue Racer, and me to Canyon Pointe. We've all given statements to the state troopers. I'm sure Trooper Hanscum can get you copies. We'll be happy to answer any further questions once the hostage situation at the Ginsburg Federal Courthouse is resolved."

The corner of Nesmith's mouth twitched. "The new head of

the local FBI office isn't allowing any supers near the site. I already called and offered our assistance."

Susan grinned. "Leave it to Harri, sir. One of our clients is a hostage."

"So is your partner Franklin." He cocked his head. "Who's Winters really worried about in there? Her partner or the perp who kidnapped her?"

"Definitely our client," Susan assured Nesmith. "If the assailants knew who they were dealing with, they wouldn't have invaded the court."

"You mean the Ghost Owl?"

"I mean all our clients with powers," Susan said sternly.

Thank goodness, the helicopter approached, kicking up wind and sand. However, stenciled on its side were the letters NSB.

Susan squinted her eyes against the blowing dirt and sand. "Where's the state trooper's helicopter?"

"We were closer." Nesmith grinned despite the dust in the air. "Besides, I owe your partners for retrieving some valuable merchandise for me. By the way, how is Harper Collins doing? I hear she's bartending down in Cabo these days."

It figured the NSB would keep an eye on Doctor Liquidation's former minion. However, Harper didn't have powers, so as long as she kept her nose clean, the NSB wouldn't mess with her. Of course, the cash the three legal partners gave the girl helped in starting a new life.

Or at least, that's what Susan hoped.

"I hear you can live pretty cheaply down in Mexico," she replied.

"You'd better get down to Canyon Point, Ms. Kennedy." Nesmith nodded toward the 'copter. "I'm looking forward to seeing part of your report on the evening news."

Susan didn't want to think about what the NSB agent meant by that as she approached the helicopter. She just prayed it didn't involve the deaths of her law partners.

CHAPTER 26

Aisha straightened and re-entered the courtroom with her hands up when Nix charged into what was left of Judge Castillo's courtroom, tailed by a squad of FBI agents. When one of the agents moved to cuff Aisha, Nix stepped between them.

"That's one of the hostages," the superhero snapped and shoved his weapon down.

"But she—" he started.

"You okay, Ms. Franklin?" Nix said, cutting off the agent. In a way, her glittery irises were reassuring through her mask.

Aisha nodded. "Besides the ones here and in the hallway overlooking the atrium, there's four more unconscious goons back in Judge Tasker's office."

"Black Falcon said he left two more in the elevator control room and a couple down in the utilities room," Nix said. "That's twenty-four. I hope we caught them all."

Dang, Rey was busy while she, Steve, and Carol were stalling Valentine.

One of the FBI agents stalked over to Aisha and Nix. "I'm Deputy Special Agent in Charge Holt. You feel up to making a statement, Ms. Franklin. Like why you're dressed as one of the terrorists?"

"First things first." Aisha crouched next to Valentine and yanked off his mask. Yep, it was definitely him. "This is Dante Valentine, AKA Crazy Jim. He was a member of the illegal black ops group Corvus. There should be a couple of warrants out for his arrest."

Holt whistled. "Is that what this was all about? Revenge on you for helping to bring down those assholes?"

Aisha straightened. "My death was just the cherry. They wanted the new Ghost Owl. Valentine's old boss, Byron Trubble has the bizarre notion that the original Ghost Owl is still alive."

Holt shrugged and holstered her weapon. "He has a point. No body was ever recovered."

"It's been a year since he was last seen falling into Lake Del Oro while battling the fake Captain Justice." Aisha chuckled weakly. "If he is still alive, he's probably on a beach in Rio. However, I'm afraid he's fish food."

"Or maybe my boss is right, and you convinced him to go legit." Holt grinned.

"I turn forty-two this year." Aisha smiled back. "I'm in decent shape, but even if I had the appropriate training, my knees and back wouldn't hold up very long fighting crime no matter what kind of powers I had . . ."

She faked sagging to the floor.

Luckily, Nix played along and grabbed her. "Aisha!"

"Sorry, it's just the stress of the day and nothing but a cup of coffee on my way here this morning," she said weakly.

"The FBI have everything under control here," Nix said. "I'll help you down to the paramedics." She looked at Holt. "If that's okay, Deputy Special Agent in Charge?"

Holt nodded. "I'll get your full statement in a little bit, Ms. Franklin."

"Thank you," Aisha said weakly. Crap, she couldn't get her own clothes, much less her purse, her tote, or her phone. Nix wrapped an arm around Aisha's shoulders and pretended to guide her out of the courtroom.

They kept the act all the way down to the main entrance. Instead of heading to one of the ambulances, Nix and Aisha wound their way to Tim's retro-fitted box truck he'd bought at a sheriff's auction. It was now the team's mobile command.

"We're approaching," Aisha said.

The right back door swung open, and Tim gave Aisha a hand up thought she didn't need it.

"Yell if you guys need something," Nix said.

Arthur monitored the activity outside on a series of monitors. Steve had already changed clothes and now sat next to Arthur. Tim shoved a bundle Aisha recognized into her arms. From the ugly expression on Tim's face, there was a lot more going on than Susan's phone exploding. It was a look only Harri could bring out of the man.

"Susan?" Aisha prompted as she started stripping off the minion's gear. Both Arthur and Steve looked away.

"Is fine," Tim said. "Steelrose wrecked Susan's rental. Mother Defiant and Blue Racer were on their way here with her. Everyone's alive though Mother Defiant has a compound fracture and Racer needed some stitches. Susan had to execute the auto-destruct in order to take out Steelrose."

"Wait, how did you talk to Susan if she doesn't have her phone?"

Aisha rose into the air a couple of inches to wiggle out of the borrowed pants.

"The three of them are in a NSB helicopter on their way to Canyon Pointe. Now that the hostage situation is over and you're alive, Susan convinced Mother Defiant to head to the hospital." Tim still had that deep furrow between his brows.

"All right, what stupid thing did your girlfriend do this time?" she asked as she pulled on her uniform pants.

"*Your* law partner is at Dewey and Cheatham," Tim growled. "She doesn't have her comm in, but Arthur's listening to what she's recording."

Aisha pulled on her jacket. "And?"

"Apparently, someone delivered a firearm to Judge Inunza this morning," Arthur said. "I believe that may have been the gunshot Susan heard over the phone when she was talking with Cobblestone, though he and Harri said they were all right.

"I called Patty. She said Harri put her and the kids on lockdown when the judge showed up at the Lechuza Building. Then Harri, Cobblestone, and the judge left in Rue Liberty's car."

"Crap," Aisha muttered. "Rue's car is too old to have GPS."

"But Harri hasn't blown up her phone yet, so we can track her with it." Arthur was starting to adopt some of Patty's chirpiness.

"That doesn't explain why she's at my former employers," Aisha pointed out.

"Susan thinks Howard Dewey is behind everything that's happened today," Tim said. "He has ties to both Corvus and the Canyon Block land deal you ladies blew up last year. He accidentally let some things slip to Mother Defiant, so Susan believes she can get a motion of summary judgment granted."

"Crap," Aisha swore. She slid on her helmet and latched it. "If Consuelo gives you a hard time, tell her you insisted I go to the hospital to be checked out."

"And if she's looking for the other you?" Tim raised an eyebrow.

"Tell her the Ghost Owl had to get a goddamn hairy kitten out of a tree."

She opened the door of the truck and launched herself into the hazy afternoon sky. Saving her best friend from her own bull-headedness was getting to be a full-time job.

CHAPTER 27

Harri and Judge Inunza darted down the hall to Howard Dewey's office. Cobblestone followed with a wailing Stuart Cheatham slung over the superhero's shoulder.

They burst into Dewey's office. He sat with Travis Beckham and Paul Inunza at the corner where the floor-to-ceiling windows met. Papers sat in front of the kid, and Paul held a pen.

"What the hell!" Dewey rose from his chair.

The judge approached his son. "Paul, please tell me you didn't sign anything."

"Dad, what are you doing here?" Paul had his father's blue-black hair but Carol's huge cinnamon eyes. He'd filled out since the last time Harri saw him. A man's build, not a kid's. His attention shifted to Harri, then to Cobblestone.

"What are *you* doing here?" the judge said. "I've been worried sick. Why did you lie to me?"

Paul jumped to his feet. "Why didn't you support Mom when she needed us most?"

Inunza grabbed the papers from the table. "Super powers? What super powers? Paul?"

"I'm sorry, Dad." The kid sadly shook his head. "I-I wanted to tell you and Mom, but after you got so upset when Captain Justice died, I couldn't."

"What superpowers do you have, Paul?" Harri asked.

"I-I can fly and kind of talk to birds," he admitted.

"You're interfering with my relationship with my client, Winters," Dewey bit out.

"It's not a client-attorney relationship when it's based on fraud," she answered. "Did you tell Paul you tried to extort his dad into killing me? Did you tell him about all your other illegal activities? Better yet, did you tell him who his biological great-grandfather was?"

Howard snorted and stuck his hands in his pants' pockets. "I have no idea what you're talking about."

Harri didn't take her eyes from Dewey. "Paul, Dewey and Cheatham handled your father's adoption fifty-five years ago." As she expected, the older attorney's jaw worked back and forth, indicating she was right.

"Adoption?" The kid faced his father. "What is she talking about, Dad?"

"My grandfather was a superhero back in his day." A slight, sad smile tilted Inunza's lips. "People were after my biological mother and me because of him. So, she put me up for adoption to protect me."

"Why haven't you ever said anything?" Paul stared at his dad with a stunned expression.

"This reunion is nice and all." Dewey smirked. "But Paul is my client, and he's a legal adult, so please leave before I call the police."

"Do it," Harri snapped. "We've got enough on you to put you away for life."

"Based on what?" Dewey sneered.

"Cheatham has already confessed to arranging for the gun sent to the judge and the threat to kill Paul if the judge didn't kill me," she growled.

"Good luck getting him on the stand," Dewey said.

"What the hell?" Cobblestone bellowed. The superhero was try to keep hold of Stuart who was convulsing. Cobblestone laid the attorney down as gently as he could. "Harri?"

The odor of burning flesh filled the office. Blood trickled from Stuart's nose. When the seizure ended, he stared at nothing.

Harri knelt next to the prone Stuart. She pressed two fingers to his neck. No pulse. This was exactly how Aisha described the death of Doctor Liquidation's second-in-command.

Cobblestone placed his hands in the CPR position on Stuart's ribcage. "I'll start chest compressions—"

Harri rested her palm on the superhero's hands. "It's over, Cobblestone." She rose to her feet and glared at Dewey. "His brain stem was just fried."

Judge Inunza pulled his son from the kid's chair and pushed Paul against the bookcase, his body between the kid and Dewey.

"What the hell is wrong with you people?" Travis jumped to feet. "You can't waltz into a law office and fry people's brains!"

"We didn't," Harri said. "Dewey did."

Travis stared at his senior partner. "Howard, what are they talking about?"

"Yeah, Howard." Harri crossed her arms. The idiot probably had another weapon on him besides the remote to kill Stuart, or he wouldn't act so cocky. "How long has your firm been in bed with

Corvus? Personally, I'd say it was from the beginning. Pablo Inunza wasn't the only baby you arranged to be adopted, was he?"

"You are grasping at straws, Harriet Mathilda." Dewey drew out the hated first and middle names.

"You may have killed Stuart, but you kill the rest of us, including your newest partner—" Harri gestured to include everybody else in the office as she took a step to her left. She needed to keep Dewey's attention on her and off the Inunzas. "—there's going to be some questions."

"Or maybe you're hyped up on cocaine like your daddy." Howard reached beneath his jacket and drew a gun. "And in your paranoid delusion, you shot the Inunzas, my colleagues, and the superhero client who tried to stop you."

"Really, Howard?" Harri shook her head. She knew her luck would eventually run out, but kicking him in the ego seemed her best distraction. "You actually have some coke stashed in here?"

Outside, sirens wailed, their rise and fall coming closer. Maybe the blonde at reception bought a clue and finally called the police.

"You'd better hurry up because if the ME doesn't find coke in my bloodstream, they'll know your story is total BS," Harri added as she stepped further to the left. As she planned, the muzzle of Dewey's gun followed her.

"I can buy and sell the ME."

"With what? The money you've skimmed from your clients?"

"Supers are so dumb." Dewey laughed "No different than any artist who sells their soul for fame."

"You said I could help people!" Paul shook with rage behind his father.

Harri wanted to scream every curse word she know as Dewey pointed his gun at the Inunzas.

"I lied." Dewey glanced at Trevor. "Well, Beckham, you said you wanted a bigger role."

"I've done shit you wanted that skated the ethical line, but I am not killing a kid or a judge on your say-so." Trevor glared at Dewey. "You're insane."

Dewey aimed his handgun at Trevor. "If you're not going to help, then you're the first—"

With a roar, Cobblestone charged. Unfortunately, he didn't have superspeed, and he plowed through Dewey's desk. It gave the corrupt lawyer time to pivot and pull the trigger.

The bullet hit Cobblestone, but this one wasn't plastic, and it obviously wasn't a normal round either. Blood sprayed from the wound, and the superhero stumbled. His size and sheer momentum carried him into the huge picture window. The reinforced glass cracked but didn't break. Cobblestone slumped to the carpet.

Travis jumped Dewey, knocking the gun out of the senior partner's hand. It bounced off the broken desk and landed on the carpet by Harri's feet. By some miracle, it didn't go off.

She grabbed the weapon, but Travis had obviously had enough. His left cross to Dewey's jaw sent the senior partner stumbling backward. He tripped over Cobblestone and smashed into the already cracked window.

For a split second, the reinforced glass appeared to hold against the older man's weight, but the whole pane crumbled. The rush of hot outdoor air took Harri's breath away. Dewey teetered at the edge before he dropped over the side of the building.

Harri cursed. Some part of her needed to look. To be sure. "No body, no death" rang through her mind.

As she tentatively approached the open space, a gray and brown figure drifted up to the level of the broken window, holding an unconscious Howard Dewey. "You people lose something?" the Ghost Owl asked.

CHAPTER 28

Susan not so patiently lay on a bed in the ER, waiting for her release paperwork. Mother Defiant and Blue Racer had threatened to call in every other superhero in Canyon Pointe to hold her down if she didn't voluntarily submit to an examination.

By some miracle, Susan hadn't broken any bones as confirmed by her head CT scan which the ER doctor insisted on after seeing the huge lump on her temple. Unfortunately, the damn scan did indicate she had a concussion.

The doctor assured her that it was a mild concussion since she only experienced dizziness and her head ached, but she hadn't lost consciousness, so her brain would recover. Which was good. It would have been very bad if she destroyed the one thing that she needed for her job.

She flipped on the TV in an attempt to distract herself.

Action 12! News's banner headline was the safe recovery of all the hostages at the Ruth Bader Ginsburg Federal Building and the apprehension of the terrorists.

"And there's another breaking story from downtown," Ted Meadowfield, the co-anchor said. "Police responded to a 9-1-1 call at the Law Offices of Dewey and Cheatham where the firm's senior partner Howard Dewey has been arrested for allegedly shooting the superhero Cobblestone among other potential charges."

The screen switched to amateur video which clearly showed the Ghost Owl catching Susan's former boss in mid-air.

"Initial reports claim Dewey may have tried to commit suicide by leaping from his office, only to be saved by the Ghost Owl, who was also instrumental in saving the courthouse hostages. We'll have more details on this developing story later tonight."

Meadowfield grinned, an obviously forced expression. "Stay tuned for a special live segment with our very own Essie Morales as she interviews local attorney Harriet Winters, the representative for the superheroes who saved so many lives at the federal courthouse this afternoon."

His grin fell, and though his microphone feed had been cut, he mouthed an obscenity a split second before the station switched to a commercial.

Susan laughed. Harri and Aisha were right. The news staff were doing everything they could to drive Meadowfield out. But it was the news anchor's own damn fault. He treated the staff like crap. Hell, he'd treated a lot of people in Canyon Pointe like crap over the years. Maybe an FCC crackdown for the mouthed swearwords would give news producer Nellie Lopez the ammunition she needed to get Meadowfield fired.

The curtain to her cubicle slid back, and one of the ER nurses entered with a handful of paperwork. "You're good to go."

Susan clicked off the TV and jumped off the gurney, but quickly realized that was a bad idea. A wave of dizziness swept through her, and she grabbed the railing to steady herself.

The nurse grabbed Susan's other arm. "This is why I'm going to wheel you out. Who's picking you up?"

"I called a taxi," Susan said as she gingerly sat on the gurney once again. Blue Racer had allowed her to borrow his phone after she'd blown up hers to take out Steelrose. "Everyone who could give me a ride is either at work or watching a bunch of kids."

The nurse pursed her lips. "Do you have someone who can stay with you in case something happens? You shouldn't be alone tonight. Not with a concussion."

"Yeah, I do." Susan smiled. "My friends will be home soon."

After going through the post-release instructions, the nurse stepped into the hallway and pushed a wheelchair into Susan's cubicle.

Once Susan was settled in the wheel chair, she looked over her shoulder at the nurse. "My clients? The supers who were brought in with me? How are they doing?"

The nurse sighed. "Legally, I can't say anything, but we can stop and see them on our way out." She winked.

"Thanks!"

After a short ride down the hall, the nurse stopped and poked her head around the curtain. "Can you handle a quick visit with your friend?"

At the murmured affirmatives, the nurse pushed back the curtain enough to wheel Susan into the cubicle. Jared wore a pair of scrubs and sat in a chair next to Eugenia's gurney. She wore a hospital gown as she lay on the thin pad. Her broken arm had been partially splinted and lightly bandaged.

"How are you two doing?" Susan asked.

"Genie's supposed to head up to surgery," Jared said. "But she got bumped back. Don't know if you heard—"

"That Cobblestone was shot this afternoon?" Susan nodded. "I didn't think bullets could penetrate his skin."

"I overheard one of the doctors say it was some kind of armor piercing bullet," Eugenia offered. "But they expect him to make a full recovery."

"That's great news! What about you guys? Do you need a place to stay?" Susan asked.

They both shook their heads.

"She'll be here at least overnight, and I'm staying with her," Jared said. "And no offense, Ms. Kennedy, we'll get our own ride back to Hermanville."

Susan laughed. "Now that's something I totally understand."

They said their goodbyes, and the nurse wheeled Susan out to the patient pickup area.

Dopinder leaned against his bright yellow taxi. Before Susan joined the firm, Harri had hired the cab driver on a monthly retainer for an anywhere, anytime pickup for the firm's personnel and their superhero clients. It was a great deal for Dopinder. He had a regular check regardless of the number of fares and a supply of superhero products for his wife and kids. Plus, the clients tipped him very well.

"Miss Susan, so nice to see you again." Dopinder opened the back passenger door for her.

"Wish it was better circumstances." She carefully got out of the wheelchair and slid into the taxi's back seat.

She thanked the nurse, and after Dopinder closed the door, she let her eyelids droop.

"I heard on the radio you, Miss Harri, and Miss Aisha had an interesting day," Dopinder said.

Susan didn't bother to open her eyes. "You could say that."

Thankfully, the cab driver remained silent the rest of the way home.

CHAPTER 29

Aisha, or rather the Ghost Owl, gave her statement to the Canyon Pointe police. She watched Travis Beckham across the room as he gave his statement to another officer. It was hard to believe that over a year ago, she had been infuriated Travis received a partnership over her. But now—

Now, she was so thankful she quit Dewey and Cheatham. She should have done it much earlier. Hell, for that matter, she should have divorced Cal much earlier.

"Is there anything else you need, Officer?" she asked politely. "Otherwise, I still need to make a statement to the FBI about the hostage rescue."

"Just one more question," he said. "How did you know what was happening here if you were down at the federal courthouse?"

"Both of Ms. Winters' partners used to work here at Dewey and Cheatham. Howard Dewey made some suspicious comments to Mother Defiant when he wooed her away from Ms. Kennedy. Mother Defiant relayed those comments to Ms. Kennedy, who then repeated them to me. The attempts on Ms. Kennedy's life and the terrorists attacking the same court in which Ms. Franklin was to appear in lead me to believe Ms. Winters was also in danger. Her head of security gave me her location from her phone's GPS. I was flying toward this building to find Ms. Winters when I saw Mr. Dewey fall."

"You say fall." The cop eyed her, or did his best since her visor was in the way. "You sure he wasn't pushed or maybe he jumped?"

Aisha shrugged. "I saw the window shatter. I saw Mr. Dewey falling. Anything else I'd say would be speculation."

The cop sighed. "That'll be all for now." He snapped his notebook shut and slapped it against his opposing palm as he glanced at Harri. "Is there a way to contact you without going through your attorneys? Since they're involved in this mess, the DA's going to be looking twice as hard at all of you."

Aisha wanted to laugh, but she couldn't. Not in front of the cop. And she sure as hell couldn't say Canyon Pointe DA Calvin Johnson was her ex-husband.

"Marta's restaurant on Sixth Street," she said. "You can leave a message with any of the employees there, and it will get to me."

The officer tipped his hat. "Thanks for your cooperation, Ghost Owl."

Aisha flew back to the federal courthouse and endured Special Agent in Charge Consuelo's tongue-lashing for taking off in the middle of an investigation. Thank god, a visor was part of her Ghost Owl costume instead of a mask. Consuelo couldn't see the faces Aisha knew she was making.

When Consuelo finally ran out of breath, Aisha said, "Howard Dewey was behind all of today's events."

Aisha laid out everything Harri and Susan had discovered. Granted it all came through Tim because neither of her partners were wearing a comm.

"And there's proof?"

"After Dewey threatened to kill Travis Beckham, too, I think you'll find he wants to be very cooperative."

"All this over a shady land deal?" Consuelo shook her head.

"There's also extortion and blackmail of judges and some questionable adoptions Dewey and Cheatham handled for Corvus," Aisha said.

"All right." Consuelo folded her arms over her chest. "Where's the original Ghost Owl?"

Would the truth satisfy the FBI agent? Time to test her and see.

"The last time I saw my predecessor, he was getting the crap knocked out of him. When he dropped into Lake Del Oro, I dove in after him." She let her voice hitch. "I couldn't find him."

"Is that why you went legit?" Consuelo appeared sympathetic.

"Partly," Aisha replied. "He also told me to register before he died. He didn't want me to make the same mistakes he did."

"You going to tell me who he was?"

"I can't," Aisha said. "I never saw his face."

Aisha couldn't handle anything more today. She avoided people by flying through the abandoned spur of the subway system to the Canyon Block and taking the old pedestrian tunnel to the Lechuza Building's underground entrance. She yanked off her glove and pressed her palm against the biometric sensor. The thick steel door whispered open.

Once the door swung shut, she unlatched her helmet and headed down to her locker room. Thanks to her new physique her mother-in-law bestowed on her, she didn't hurt anywhere. She was just bone tired.

The intercom buzzed. Aisha pressed the button. "It's just me, Patty."

Their assistant's breath whistled through the receiver. "Just making sure. Harri has Rue's car, so I'm giving her the keys to my minivan. Rue didn't want to leave until you, Rey, or Steve got home. Arthur and I can exchange and pick up everyone's cars tomorrow."

"That sounds great." Aisha leaned against the wall. "Anything else?"

"Susan's got a concussion. I'll stay with her tonight, but she wants you to debrief her before she forgets something. If it helps, I'll bring a bottle of wine."

Aisha chuckled. "You're on. Let me shower and change. How's Mitch?"

Her son gurgled in the background. "He's darn close to sitting up on his own. You may want to take a day or two off and spend it with him."

The guilt of career versus family hit Aisha harder than one of Steve's punches. Add in the superheroing thing, and she definitely wasn't spending enough time with her son.

"That's good advice. I may just take you up on it."

"One other thing." Patty sighed. "Harri agreed to a live interview here, and the Action 12! News truck just parked in front of our building."

"Thanks for the update." Aisha made a fist, but she forced herself to relax. No sense destroying the team's property. She gently pressed the intercom's off button.

However, she was too damn tired to cover Harri's ass yet again. If her partner made the deal, she needed to live up to it.

CHAPTER 30

Harri spotted the news truck as she turned onto Sixth Street. Damn, she'd totally forgot about her interview with Essie. Thankfully, Judge Inunza called a rideshare. He and Paul were going home to discuss the future over pizza.

Surprisingly, Travis Beckham apologized to Paul for being conned by Howard Dewey. Now, that the kid's secret was out, maybe things would get better for the Inunza family.

The judge was even considering issuing a formal statement regarding his biological grandfather, Eagle Forever.

Harri pulled into the Lechuza Building's garage and parked in one of the visitor spots. She grabbed her brush out of her purse and redid her ponytail before she swiped on some lipstick. It would have to do for this interview. She locked up Rue's antique sedan and strode down to where Essie and the cameraman Bob were set up.

"I was beginning to think you'd forgotten." Essie grinned.

"No, I didn't," Harri lied. "I got hung up by police questioning me since I was in Howard Dewey's office when he shot Cobblestone." At least, that part was true.

"Wait." Essie waved her left hand because the heavy microphone was in her right. "I thought you were at the federal courthouse now that the hostages were released."

Harri held up her palms. "Look, I haven't had one second to even glance at your proposed questions. Let's roll, and I'll answer all your questions as best as I can."

Essie nodded and touched her own earpiece. "You got that, Jenny?"

"We're ready," Bob said. "The station is cutting to us in five, four . . ." He ticked off the last three seconds with his fingers only before he pointed at Essie.

"This is Essie Morales, coming to you live in front of the Lechuza Building. Here with me is senior partner of Winters and Franklin, Harri Winters."

Harri tried for a mix of confidence and pleasantry. "Thank you, Essie."

"Your partner, Aisha Franklin, was one of the hostages at the federal courthouse today. How is she doing after her release?"

"She's shaken but unharmed. I have to give credit to the fantastic response by the FBI in this situation. Together, they and several of the city's superheroes rescued all forty-seven hostages with only two casualties."

"And the two casualties?" Essie prompted.

"A security guard at the Ginsburg Federal Courthouse and the bailiff in Judge Francis Castillo's court. Both were shot by the terrorists, but last I heard, both were in serious but stable condition."

"Franklin was representing Carol Inunza at her arraignment this morning," Essie continued. "Inunza was accused of kidnapping you and being a co-conspirator in the Mauvaises Prison breakout last month. Why would Franklin represent Inunza after what she did to you?"

"I've known the Inunza family a long time," Harri said. "Carol is going through some personal problems. While I don't condone her actions regarding the breakout, she still deserves adequate representation and getting the support she needs."

As Harri expected, Essie switched subjects to the more current news topic. "I understand you were a witness to the alleged shooting of Cobblestone by local attorney Howard Dewey. Can you tell our viewers what happened?"

"Unfortunately, I can't go into too many details. This is an open investigation by the Canyon Pointe Police Department. However, I can confirm Cobblestone was shot this afternoon. The last word I got a half hour ago was he is in surgery, but he's expected to make a full recovery."

"Did Howard Dewey try to commit suicide this afternoon?" Essie's eyes gleamed from getting this scoop.

"No. There was a struggle when another partner at Dewey and Cheatham Travis Beckham tried to get the gun from Howard Dewey. Travis managed to knock the gun away. Howard tripped over Cobblestone's body, and he hit a window that had already been damaged. It shattered and he fell." Harri shook her head. "Thank goodness, the Ghost Owl was there to catch him."

"Is it true Dewey killed another employee at the firm?"

Harri hesitated. "That's for the ME to determine, not me. I can verify he was not shot like Cobblestone was."

"What caused Dewey to resort to violence?"

"That's what the CPPD investigation will reveal," Harri said firmly.

"Can you give us a hint?" Essie pleaded.

"Once things are confirmed, you'll be the first to know."

Essie turned to the camera. "This is Essie Morales reporting from the Lechuza Building on Sixth Street. Back to Ted at the studio."

Harri held her pleasant expression until Bob signaled the interview was over. She turned to Essie. "I'm sorry I can't tell you more right now. Last thing I want is to ruin the case the DA's building."

"Can I ask you something off the record?" Essie said while Bob started packing up their equipment.

"Sure," Harri said.

"Dewey killed Stuart Cheatham because he was about to rat Dewey out, didn't he?"

Harri nodded. "I'm afraid so. But it's up to the detectives and the DA's office to build that case. Otherwise, Dewey's going to walk."

"I had a friend who used to work at that firm." Essie shook her head and she stared at the concrete. "The stories she told me . . ." Essie stared directly in Harri's eyes. "Those asshats need to go down."

"I totally agree—shit!" Harri dug out the keys for Rue's antique sedan. "I promised to meet someone. Sorry, but I gotta go."

Essie waved as Harri whirled and raced for the garage. "See you later!"

⁓

Harri screeched to a halt in front of Marta's restaurant and ran inside to the owner sitting at the register. "There's a girl I sent here—"

"She's here." Marta beckoned Harri to follow her. She led Harri to the tiny closet that was her office. Marta hesitated at the door. "I told her Cheatham was dead. That seemed to help her mood a little."

Harri nodded and opened the door. Marta's trash can overflowed with used tissues. The girl sitting at Marta's desk jumped.

"Hey, Deedee." Harri eased the door closed. "How are you doing?"

"Besides my job being threatened if I didn't suck Slimy Stuart's dick, embarrassing myself in front of a judge I respect, and losing my job all in one day." The girl sniffed. "I'm doing just peachy."

Harri perched her hip on the corner of Marta's desk. "Do you have someone at home? Or someone who could stay with you tonight?"

Deedee shook her head. "I moved here for my internship with Judge Inunza. I really liked Canyon Pointe, so when I got the offer from one of the most prestigious firms in the country, I thought I had it made."

Harri's phone rang. She checked the caller ID. It was Patty. "I'm sorry but I need to take this," Harri said to Deedee before she thumbed the answer button. "What do you need? I'm in the middle of something."

"You finished the interview. We were watching. Could you pick up our order at Marta's?" Patty enunciated carefully.

"Are you drunk?" Harri asked.

"Not yet, but Aisha and I are on our way. Susan can't drink because of her concussion."

"What concussion?" Harri said. "Susan was fine after this morning's accident."

"Shhh! Not so loud," Patty said louder than Harri. "The babies are sleeping."

"Give the phone to Aisha," Harri ordered.

In the background, Patty said, "Mommy's pissed."

"Hey, Harri." Aisha didn't sound as intoxicated as Patty. "We're in Susan's apartment for the post-crisis breakdown. I put in an order for you at Marta's, too."

"I bringing someone with me." Harri took a deep breath and released it. "You remember Becky Roth?"

"Yeah. The receptionist at Dewey and Cheatham who had the balls to nail those bastards for sexual harassment."

Harri looked at Deedee. Tears were running down the girl's face again. "I've got a friend with a similar problem."

"Bring her over," Aisha said. "We'll share food and tequila and help her take the rest of that screwed up firm down."

CHAPTER 31

Aisha led the round of applause at Harri's first successful interview since forming the partnership when their senior partner arrived with the food and another wayward soul.

Brainstorming Deedee's legal moves helped Aisha forget her own exhaustion. Or it did until someone knocked on Susan's apartment door.

"Crap," Harri muttered. "I hope we didn't wake up Grace."

Aisha rose to answer the door. When she opened it, it wasn't an irate Arthur with a crying Grace. It was Rey with Special Agent in Charge Consuelo.

"What happened?" Adrenaline rushed through Aisha's blood as she looked at one, then the other. It ended on her husband. "You didn't leave Mitch upstairs alone?"

"Give me a little credit," Rey growled. "Steve's with him. But you're the lawyer." He pointed at Consuelo. "You need to fix this. Now." He stomped toward the elevator.

"Let's go downstairs to my office," Aisha said.

"Nah," Consuelo walked inside like she owned the place. "After the day we've had, I could use some tequila and food, too." She plopped down on the couch next to Harri. "For those of you, I haven't met yet, I'm Sylvia."

"Translated, that means she's Special Agent in Charge Sylvia Consuelo, the new head of the Canyon Pointe FBI office," Harri said sourly.

"But why are you here?" Susan asked.

"I wanted a little face-to-face with the real Ghost Owl." Consuelo picked up a loaded nacho and shoved it into her mouth.

"Really?" Aisha bit out. "I heard the police tried to bypass his attorneys by telling him they needed an alternate contact."

"That didn't come from my office," Consuelo pointed out.

"Wait a minute, Special in Charge Agent Sylvia." Patty waved her hands. "We're in the middle of a consultation."

"Looked like a girls' night to me." Consuelo selected a chicken taquito and swirled it through the guacamole.

"Then I'll arrange a face-to-face tomorrow," Aisha said coolly.

Consuelo calmly chewed her taquito before she answered, "You're getting sloppy, Ghost Owl. If a grunt like me can figure it out, then anyone can. You're putting your family at risk."

"What?" Aisha played up her fake confusion, but the truth was on everyone's faces. Except poor Deedee, whose eyes grew big and round.

Consuelo grabbed another taquito and waved it at Aisha. "You're a decent actor, girlfriend, but your partners suck."

"I'm not your girlfriend," Aisha snapped.

"Look, I'm not here to harass you. I'd like a decent working relationship with the superheroes in Canyon Pointe." Consuelo dipped the second taquito in the guacamole. "This was the first hostage situation were either one my people or one of the hostages didn't get killed because of supers." She shrugged. "I'm willing to keep an open mind if you are."

Aisha exchanged looks with Harri, who gave her a we-can-try hand wave.

"You have got to tell me where to get these," Consuelo said around her mouthful of chicken, tortilla, and guacamole. "They taste like the ones my abuelita used to make."

"A place called Marta's," Susan said. "Three blocks east on Sixth."

Consuelo rose. "Like I said, I only wanted to give you a heads up. Be careful out there, Ghost Owl. And I truly am sorry about your mentor." She clapped Aisha on the shoulder as she passed.

After Consuelo closed the door, Aisha shut her eyes and listened. Rey waited at the elevator to escort the FBI agent down to the first floor. Damn, there was going to be a serious discussion when she got home.

"Are—are you really the Ghost Owl?" Deedee said.

"No," Aisha snapped.

"But you know who is." the girl said.

"The Owl's my client," Susan said. "And yes, I do know. But for your own sake, don't ask us anymore questions."

Deedee made a sound low in her throat. "I'm going to do my best to forget everything here." She made another sound, this time a sob. Patty scooted closer and hugged the girl.

"What do you want, Deedee?"

She sniffed. "I think I want to go home to Utah. Maybe go back to school." She reached for a tissue and blew her nose. "I guess I want a little time to figure out my next step."

"I'll call Travis tomorrow," Aisha said. "Given the circumstances, I think we can get you a little seed money to give you that time."

CHAPTER 32

A knock on her office door drew Rue Liberty's attention from the picture on her computer screen. She tapped a key to show the screen saver before she said, "Come in."

The door opened, and Pablo Inunza strode into the room.

"Well?" she said.

"Your plan worked," he said. "Winters, Franklin, and Kennedy took the bait."

"It did kill the proverbial two birds." Rue smiled. "Luckily, Dewey's full of himself and said too much to poor, sweet Mother Defiant."

Inunza sat in one of the chairs on the other side of Rue's desk. "Those ladies aren't going to be distracted forever. No matter how many times you play sweet little old grandmother to their kids. They're too damn smart."

"Then get your wife under control," she said mildly.

"Your daughter was just as guilty about screwing up the jailbreak," he shot back.

"True." Rue sighed. "It's unfortunate the Ghost Owl saw Monica leave with Trubble."

"You can't keep playing both sides, Prudence." He shook his

head. "The entire Winters and Franklin team has been the Ghost Owl at one point or another, and they each have a piece of the puzzle. Eventually, they will put everything together."

"I just need them off both of our asses a little longer. Thanks to your so-called stress-induced bad judgment, they won't give you a second thought." She set her elbows on her desk and rested her chin on her clasped hands. "Trubble's close to breaking."

"And if he doesn't?"

"There are other avenues I'm pursuing."

He tilted his head. "If you're sure?"

"I'm sure," she said.

Once he left and closed the door behind him, she tapped the key to clear the screen saver. A black and white mugshot of Timothy Mitchell Canyon stared back at her.

"The real question is what's your involvement in the missing children, my dear original Ghost Owl."

Distractions? How about a family wedding? The team heads to Atlanta for the nuptials of Aisha's baby brother, but it may be the bride and groom who has to save the superheroes' collective bacon.

Turn the page for a sneak peak of
A Very Hero Wedding!

A Very Hero Wedding

The heat inside the Lechuza Building didn't match the last blaze of sweltering summer in Canyon Pointe. No, the heat inside was much worse despite the chilled air pumping from the building's ancient ventilation system. Nor could it be soothed by the iced version of Aisha Franklin's favorite no-fat, sugar-free peppermint mocha.

As much as she wanted to see her blood kin at her baby brother's wedding, she wished she could leave her adopted family behind. She glared at her law partner and best friend, Harri Winters, who sat across their office conference room table.

"We need someone to cover the office. We can't leave for a week with no one—" Aisha began.

Again.

"Then find someone we can trust!" Harri yelled.

"I said I would stay—" Susan Kennedy, their third and newest partner, started to say.

"No!" Aisha and Harri shouted at the same time.

Loud banging filled the room before Patty Ames, their legal assistant and all-around Girl Friday, shoved the door open. Blue eyes blazed from beneath her wayward blond curls. "Keep it down in here. The clients on the phone can hear you."

Patty didn't yell. She used what their building manager's four sons referred to as her "Mommy-growly" voice. Not even Aisha's husband Rey or her brother-in-law Steve messed with Patty when she used that voice, and they were both supers.

"We're sorry," Aisha said. "We'll be quieter."

"Harri?" Patty's voice carried an obvious warning. Ever since her daughter Grace was born, their assistant acted more and more like the firm's boss.

Or the partners' mother.

"I'll be quiet, Patty," Harri grumbled.

"Thank you." Patty closed the conference room door behind her.

"All I'm saying is opposing counsel will use the opportunity of the office being closed to pull shenanigans," Aisha said.

"Because that's what you'd do," Harri snapped.

"Isn't that the pot calling the kettle black?" Susan asked. When Aisha glared at her, Susan held up her palms. "Was that racist? I swear I wasn't going there."

Aisha blew out a deep breath and decided to ignore the jibe. "Too bad Steve isn't licensed yet. We could stick him with desk duty as the newbie."

"Why don't we?" Susan said. "He's not going to Martin's wedding because of classes. He's taking the legal clinic at the law school next year. Let's give him the experience. If something happens and he needs a licensed attorney, he can call one of us."

Aisha exchanged looks with Harri. "It's a good idea. I'll fly home if there's a major problem."

"You can't," Harri said. "It's your brother's wedding."

"You can't," Aisha replied. "It's your foster brother's wedding."

Susan waved her arms. "Excuse me! I said I would stay from the beginning."

"Shhhhh!" Aisha and Harri said at the same time.

Harri glanced over her shoulder, but the conference room door didn't open. She looked at Susan. "You don't want her back in here, yelling at us, do you?"

"So, we're agreed?" Aisha said. "Steve handles the phones except when he's in class?"

"What about when he's not in class?" Harri asked.

"What about Javier's friend Josie?" Aisha suggested.

Harri shook her head. "She's finally back in high school. I don't mind giving her odd jobs around the building on the weekends and summer, but I am not giving her an excuse to drop out. What about her mom Veronica? Javier said something about her losing her job again."

Aisha slowly nodded. "Yeah, that might work." Like a lot of people in the neighborhood, Veronica had grabbed her kids and fled north because of trouble in Central America. In their case, Veronica's family had immigrated legally. However, Veronica had a lot of trouble getting her teaching certification in the U.S. She fell into a downward spiral her pride and American prejudice wouldn't let her pull out of. Maybe this was a chance to do some good. "I'll talk to her."

"I can do it," Harri said.

"Your Spanish sucks," Aisha and Susan said in unison.

"She's going to need to speak English when answering the phone," Harri snapped.

"She's going react more positively to someone she thinks is one of her own," Aisha said. "Someone who speaks like a native. Do you realize you have a British accent when you speak Spanish?"

"I've been—" Harri started loudly. When Aisha hissed and pointed at the door, Harri lowered the volume of her voice. "I've been practicing."

"I'll talk with Veronica," Aisha insisted.

"You mean the Ghost Owl will talk with Veronica." Harri crossed her arms and sulked.

"The Ghost Owl will get through to her better than a bunch of stuck-up gringa lawyers," Susan said.

"She's got a point," Aisha said.

"Fine," Harri said while she stood. "Anything else we need to talk about?"

Both Aisha and Susan shook their heads.

"Fine," Harri repeated before she stomped out of the conference room.

"What the hell crawled up her butt?" Susan muttered. "It's just a wedding. I'm not even sure why your brother invited me."

"This isn't about the wedding," Aisha replied.

"You've got to be kidding me." Susan flopped against the back of her chair and rolled her eyes. "This is still about the Paris thing?"

"Unfortunately." Aisha tapped her nails against the conference table. Harri better get her shit sorted before they flew to Atlanta on Friday for Martin's wedding.

Otherwise, Aisha might just drop her best friend from thirty thousand feet.

———— •••• ————

Acknowledgements

This is for all of the survivors of the COVID-19 pandemic who bought my books to help keep their sanity in these trying times. Thank you for helping me keep mine by focusing on the stories.

Suzan Harden transitioned from writing information technology manuals for companies and legal articles for a law enforcement magazine to her first love, fantasy and science fiction in all their forms. She's the author of the Bloodlines, the 888-555-HERO, and the Justice series.

www.ingramcontent.com/pod-product-compliance
Lightning Source LLC
Chambersburg PA
CBHW071003180726
48291CB00004B/1417